An Evening with Mrs. Eugenia Nwafor:

Mrs. Eugenia Nwafor was in the kitchen. She was in a flurry of activity, as she always was in the evening, on arriving from her offices at the Department of Agriculture. On this evening in particular, her face appeared irritated, and there was heaviness in her step, as she twirled from the chopping board to the stove top.
 She was dressed in her wrapper and a green scarf. It was a relief to have put aside her girdle and the western skirt and blouse, which somehow never seemed to fit her properly; if it had once done so, then that must have been a long time ago. The skirt rode up on her bulging abdomen, and the blouse which buttoned up the front always displayed undue tension at the buttons, ready to give way at the slightest provocation. As best she could she tried to disguise all this with a large black jacket. She wore it over her bulky frame every day. Wrappers could fit anybody, in so far as the material was long enough.

In a corner of the kitchen Donatus the houseboy cowered sheepishly on a chair by the kitchen table, and watched the familiar activity which by now he had long since become accustomed to. His own part in the performance had already been played out much earlier when he had spent the better part of the afternoon prepping the ingredients for Oga's chop.
"Frrrresh soup, frrrresh soup, everrrry day" were the now famous watchwords of Christian Nwafor, and as he said this he would roll his r's really loud so as to emphasize to all, that in this house no substitute would be acceptable.
"What did I marry a wife for, if she cannot provide fresh food every day?"
 He was often quoted as lamenting to his friends at the bar.
 And then, there was what he had proclaimed so brazenly to his wife during the first week
of their marriage, as she had unwisely attempted to serve him the previous day's leftovers.
 "Fresh soup, Madam, please." He had told her. "I only eat frrresh soup everyday."

And the rest is history. For the next nineteen years of their marriage, she may have failed him in many regards. But in that regard she had wisely complied, and had never failed to produce a bowl of steaming soup directly from the pot to the table; with a mound of pounded yam, always on its own plate beside it.

As such, although Donatus could assist in the prepping of the ingredients, the unwritten rule was that it was the hand of Mrs. Eugenia which had to throw these ingredients into the pot. It was, however, acceptable for Donatus to stir the pot, until more ingredients needed to be added.

Later on, emanating from the kitchen was the "Kthow kthow" as the yam was pounded in the wooden mortar into a paste.

By the time Mr Christian ate his dinner it was usually quite late and as such he ate alone and in complete silence.

"Many a day I have wondered," Mrs. Eugenia would think to herself.
"What if one day, I was not here when he came back, or I served him old food?

"Or, if Donatus put the ingredients in the pot, and not me? Would he really know the difference?"

But all these were distant thoughts, which were indulged in rarely.

There had been a time when she had cared very much about what or how Christian felt. With time she had discovered, that unlike what happened in the Mills and Boons novels of her youth, her feelings did not seem to carry any significant weight with her spouse. Indeed it would not be entirely wrong to assert that they were blatantly ignored.

After years of this neglect she had come to face what mattered to her truly, and that was the fate of her four children.

There were four of them and she duly obsessed about their welfare. What they did or did not do; and what they ate or did not eat. She worried about what they would one day become. With the same diligence she tried to predict their every need and desire, and fulfill them all in so far as it was within her power and her limited means to. Somehow, they made her life livable and had become her one and only raison d'être.

Every salary she received from the Department of Agriculture as office manager for the permanent secretary went into shoes, clothing, school fees and sundry expenditures on their behalf.

During the school year they were all boarders, and after dinner she would retreat into her room by herself and obsess over them, one by one.

Chinedu was the first born and her oldest son, followed by Afam also a boy, then the two little girls Henrietta and Christiana.

For three years Chinedu had been the only issue, and he had seemed to have been teetering on deaths door. As a consequence of this she had always had an undue partiality towards him.

She had nearly despaired of having any further children when in the fourth year of her marriage, just as Christian was getting "serious" with his mistress Henrietta, seemingly by divine providence, she became taken in. It was only the arrival in quick succession of Afam, and then the two girls that had saved her marriage.

To add insult to injury, despite the violent opposition of his wife, when his first daughter had been born he had given her the name of his mistress. Her relatives had calmed her down with:

"Put up a fight, and he'll throw you out for sure... and bring Henri in…"

In consequence of this she had decided to suffer in silence.

Not even the births of all the children had put a damper on his affair with his mistress, whom he unfailingly visited every night.

All this Mrs. Eugenia had faced with great courage and resilience; she had tried to look at the positive things in her life, and not at all the things which were glaringly absent. At times she had regretted not having had a soul mate for a husband, instead of this distant figure, or gestalt that came and left at will. But when she compared her life with the life of her friends she realized it was not so bad at all; in so far as she lacked for none of the basic necessities of daily living, she was doing very well.

Most people, she thought, put on a front about how rosy their lives were; when in fact no one really knew what was going on behind those walls of the home.

"Show me," she had addressed her dear sister Margaret "The husband who can stay in love with his wife and you have shown me a saint."

This was barely an excuse for Christian's behavior which could only be described as despicable. Try as Margaret might to point this out to her older sister, her sister had adamantly refused to acknowledge any irregularity in her precarious home situation. The last thing in

the world she intended to do was to deliver Christian into the arms of Henri. They would have to wait until she died, literally.
Christian himself was well aware of his wife's attitude. Fully recognizant of her helplessness in the present ongoing situation he made no effort to hide his nefarious activities. He would even have discussed his mistress with her, if she would give him audience, which she wisely would not.

Hence, the two made great effort to avoid each other, at all times, and under all circumstances. Messages were sent back and forth with the children or with Donatus and even these, only when absolutely necessary.

"When we married at first I had truly been in love," she had explained to her sister,
"But see what has happened now, he never seeks me out anymore. He never bothers with my feelings or if I have all I need. It is hard to stay in such a marriage without feeling victimized and abused."
Such a mindset never helped to instill harmony in a home that lacked it in the first place. And Christian went about his own business in total disregard for her. He was a religious man of sorts, and did not consider the taking of a mistress to be good in and of it self. Yet, he now found himself increasingly powerless over the control of this emotion and the affair. It had become as much a part of him as his leg or his arm. And how can a man cut off his arm?

Over the ensuing years the desire to regularize his mistress's situation became more intense, mainly at her behest. Henrietta felt that as long as he went home to his wife every evening, he did not truly belong to her.

The first step was the traditional wedding which was presently in the offing.

Although great care had been taken to keep the matter from his wife, this little piece of information had been leaked to her. Initially, she had decided to ignore this, in the belief that opposition on her part would only serve the purpose of driving the errant spouse deeper into the arms of her rival. Thus, on this evening in question she had decided to wait in the living room until her husband's return, and to make an attempt at a connection.

She sat herself on the sofa with her Bible in her lap and with the green scarf neatly tied and retied nervously around her head she awaited the arrival of Christian. On the table sat a large dish of soup. The soup was his favorite ogbonno soup. .

A little after ten p.m. he walked in with his shirt rumpled and his tie off.

He was surprised to see her waiting for him and realized immediately that something was very wrong.

"Good evening," He greeted her. With more of the tone one would use on a stranger than on one's own wife. "How are you today?" He asked.

Eugenia forced a smile as she looked up from her Bible

"Good evening. How was your day?" She said with the most pleasant tone she could muster.

He did not answer the question but instead sat down and started to wash his hands in the bowl of water left on the table for him to wash in, and started to eat his food unceremoniously.

"I asked you how was your day?" She repeated still in a soft tone.

He looked up from his bowl of soup with a puzzled look on his face. "Oh sorry, I missed that; yes I had a very good day, I try to always have a good day". He replied dryly.

"Or, are you able to make a bad day good? " She asked.

He shrugged and went back to eating.

She obviously had an agenda, and he had no intentions of playing it out her way. If she wanted to play it out she would have to do this unprompted by him.

"I always try myself to make a bad day good myself…" She said. And he still did not answer.

 She continued,

" Lately, everyday has been bad but I try to say nothing; thinking it will all sooner or later turn out alright, but so far nothing has changed :"

"Are you referring to your work or are you referring to me?" He finally answered.

"I'm sorry, but I don't quite understand the purpose of this conversation, Eugenia. You never wait up for me. What do you want?"

"That is not true; I always wait up for you." She cried out, "Maybe not physically in this living room but I hear all your comings and your goings. I know when and how late you come back, and I know where you come from."

He laughed, and continued with a sneer,

"How can you know where I come from? Where I go is no secret. If I come from anywhere, it is not a secret. And maybe if you had been more of a caring wife, all this would have never happened."

"Would have never happened?" she said with agitation. "Christian, was it I who drove you? Or was it you who drove yourself? How dare you to blame me for your own weaknesses!"

Without a further word he rose from his chair at the dining table. He walked past her and closing the door firmly behind him vanished into his bedroom.

She broke down in tears right where she was seated on the sofa in the living room. Unable to control her emotions, she buried her face in the sofa cushion and wept, muffling her cries with the cushioning. She had never really thought that any attempts on her part to repair the broken relationship would have any effect on her husband. But nevertheless, she had decided that she would try. Even if only to assuage her conscience, that she had done all possible to diminish the rift that separated them. As she wept her heart out, it became unclear to her what she was weeping for. It could just have well been for the pain of rejection or for the pain of loss, which had never felt as acute as now on the day before the eve of his traditional wedding.

After the passage of a fair amount of time she got up from the sofa and straightened out her wrapper and pulling her shoulders back she stood upright and went quietly into her room.

The next step had been rehearsed in her mind countless times. In the event of failure, rather than stay with a man who had taken on a new wife, she had decided to take what little there was left of her self esteem and leave while she still could. That night she stayed up until the early hours of the morning. Her trunk of wrappers was packed. In the old brown suitcase her father had given her when she had started university she had packed the remainder of her clothes.

In a little cardboard box she had packed up the few mementoes of her children, little photos and trivia.

By dawn a Taxi had been called. Before her husband could even awaken she had left, leaving behind her the little room as neat as she had met it.

Donatus had cried and begged her not to go; he also begged to know where she was going. Being intent on leaving behind as little information about herself as possible she whispered a word into Donatus ear at which point he managed to stop from further crying and seemed reassured that his dear madam would be fine.

As she drove in the Taxi the driver took her to Asata to her sister's house. She watched as the little houses flashed by and here and there some early risers were already on their way to market. It had been nineteen years of misery, and she could hardly believe that it was all over. Sixteen years it had taken her to pick up the courage and to leave, to finally capitulate to Henri.

"Let her win." She said to herself, "nothing is quite worth this sorrow."

There was no need to be sitting and waiting for a situation to turn itself around when obviously it was over. Sheer persistence had not been enough. It was not that she lacked love for this her dear husband, more that SHE DID NOT KNOW HOW TO EXPRESS IT. AND WAS NEVER GIVEN THE OPPORTUNITY TO DO THE SAME.

.

Life in Asata:

Comfort lived in Asata with her family in a small flat in a house of larger size. The house was built to surround a central courtyard. There were kitchens on the outside of the courtyard where food could be prepared using firewood and some cement blocks placed to form a base. The building itself was of shabby construction with walls some straight and others not quite so. The exterior which was made of a layer of cement belied the fact that the walls were made of native construction with red mud, and merely reinforced by an exterior layer of cement. The layer of cement was itself stained in many places with reddish brown dust. In this part of the town the houses were built close in a haphazard manner with no real roads only dirt paths which served as roads.

Comfort was startled to see her sister approaching their modest apartment with a trunk, a big suitcase and the brown cardboard box. Her initial thought was that perhaps something drastic had happened; as perhaps Mr. Nwafor had died or had had a stroke, etc.
She dropped the grinding stone she was using to grind beans for akara, and ran to meet her older sister and to assist her with the load. "Sister, it is early for you to be on the road with so many luggages." She said, too frightened to ask directly the reason for this.
Mrs. Nwafor nodded in assent.
"Eh". she answered , "I have had enough. I have left. Today is the day before his marriage to Henrietta and I have decided to make it on my own"
.

Her sister moaned, "Sister, that IS THE WORST THING YOU COULD EVER DO! Do you know what the society thinks of divorced women? You will never remarry!"
Mrs. Eugenia was aghast in disbelief and responded:
"Hum, I am not looking to remarry. I am not trying to please a world that has no knowledge of the sorrows that I bear. All this while, I stayed for the sake of my children. But now that my children are big enough it is okay for me to leave. No need to sit and wait for a man who has gone".
At this juncture they had reached the backdoor, and they proceeded to drag the suitcase in and place it in the middle of the one room that Comfort shared with her entire family. It was in this one room they ate and slept and read their books. One window was shuttered with burglar proofing.
The room was stuffy after the long night and all who had slept in there.
"How long will you stay?" Comfort asked trying not to seem too concerned.

Her sister answered:
"I will only be here for one night. I hope to stay with my friend Mrs. Chijioke. She is widowed. Right now she is out of town, she will not be back until tomorrow and then I can leave you."
She continued,"I must go to work now, and I will look for you in the evening At the Market place"

Being in danger of running late to work, she quickly assembled her hand bag and fixed herself up by applying a small dab of white powder to conceal the shininess of her face. With a small rag she dusted off her shoes which had become dusty after the walk and left for her office.
Comfort was looking after her with a puzzled look. Although she had said nothing, it was peculiar that after sixteen years of dating his mistress that only now should Mrs. Eugenia decide to leave. Nevertheless, Comfort was not one to spend much of her time worrying about the misfortunes of others. She was consumed by her own fate, and the fact that misfortune was always on the horizon in her own home in some form or the other. Being the mother of five children there was always enough sickness to go around. Near misses with death were as real as life itself. How many times had they not been in with fever or malaria or diarrhea? Sometimes the food was not enough if her husband had had a bad day at work. Sometimes there was no money for school fees and the children had to take a little note to school appealing to the principal to 'please let them stay', as they would 'pay the next week'... And when this had failed they had often relied on the kindness of Mrs. Eugenia herself who would pay the school fees in the event that all else had failed.

Mrs. Eugenia was a firm believer in education.
"Whatever happens, do not let the children drop out of school." She had begged Comfort, who had frequently been tempted to just give up on the idea of educating her children.
At one point she had wanted her eldest daughter Regina to help her at the market with the stall that she kept, as that would have considerably made her life easier. Regina was a bright student. After much pleading from Mrs. Eugenia, she was now away at commercial school, herself trying to learn how to become a secretary. All the other children were still young and in primary and

secondary school and it was still too early to predict how well they would do.

"This life, Oh!" Comfort said, to herself. "Sometimes I do not understand it at all… The trouble between a man and wife, that, no one can ever understand."
She put away the beans she was grinding and gathered her little bag and put on her rubber slippers. Tied her wrapper and her scarf and set out for her stall. She was the poorest of all the sisters, "But dear me!" she said to herself, and thought,
her husband still loved her; and her children were obedient, and all were at present in good health. There were some things that money could not buy.
"For all the money in the world and all the things that Mrs. Eugenia has… She does not have a husband who loves her; in fact, she may not even have a husband at all right now." She mumbled to herself. "After all, they will say that she is the one who left. And after you have left there is no saying that if you change your mind that you will be able to get back in. So why leave in the first place?" She went on thinking to herself, "Unless you are absolutely sure that you're not going back."
There was little or no room for any other thought on this matter to the mind of Comfort. So firmly did she believe in the institution of marriage, and so poorly did she think of the alternative of the lack of it that she could not even imagine life without a husband.

The same evening that Mrs. Eugenia left, Henrietta moved her belongings in unceremoniously.
The pictures left behind on the wall of Mrs. Eugenia and her husband, remembrances of better days were swiftly removed. And indeed it would have been impossible to ascertain without prior knowledge that Mrs. Eugenia Nwafor had ever lived there at all, for so thoroughly were all traces of her removed from the house.

"They change the wives like they are changing the cloth". Comfort grumbled to herself, as she arranged her wares for the day in her little stall at Ogbete Market
. "No loyalty in this world. What has this world become? And the women where do they come from? Surely they too must know that

these men are taken. But to them all this counts for nothing. No religion!"

Comfort was nervous about the evening. To say the least, her accommodations were hardly adequate for her immediate family, and there really was no space for any additional person.
 Later that evening, the sight of Mrs. Eugenia approaching her stall in the market was enough to bring her to tears. Her ungainly form waddled her way forward in her usual manner, but her head which was usually upright and stood tall was now stooped over and bent. As if by looking down at the red earth somehow the world would forget her sorrows; or better still change everything, and make everything good again. What ever good was, for she had not known a good life, for so long; that it seemed as a reverie, an unattainable goal.
Or erstwhile a good life was a goal to be reached, by others, but never by her.
 The skirt rode up over her mid section as she walked and she pulled the skirt down yet again.

Dinnertime in Asata:

The evening had arrived suddenly while they were on their way home by bus.
 One moment, it was light and within the span of minutes the sun was setting over the Milliken hills which were standing tall and dark in the distance.
 With the setting of the sun a nice cool breeze wafted in through the bus window; a welcome relief to all, after the stifling heat of the day.

Comfort was in a good mood. She had had a comparatively good day at her stall where she sold Ankara cloths.

Business life had its ups and downs. Christmas and Easter were the two boom periods, and in between there were a sprinkling of customers, which could be more irregular than regular. Nevertheless, she was grateful to her dear husband for having set her up in business; as for the most part she could cover the school fees and incidental expenses from her business.

Mrs. Eugenia's mood had experienced no elevation whatsoever. As the day had worn on, her depression had deepened even more. More, and more, the gravity of her situation had become clearer to her. To think, that she had given up so easily after so long tolerating the situation. But then now it was too late, and nothing could change the present situation.

By the time they arrived at Comfort's home it was pitch black. From the main road there was no further lighting on the side street as they made their way down the unpaved road. They progressed carefully, avoiding gutters that served as sewage drainage and jumping over gully's left over from the rains, which had unrelentingly marked long and deep grooves down the hills.

Within the house all were already seated at the table with Moses at the head and were eating garri with egusi soup from their individual plastic bowls.

"Ndewo." they greeted them. Moses stood up and welcomed his wife and her sister.

"Mrs. Eugenia, it is always a pleasure to see you." He said hesitatingly, not knowing what really to say in the present situation.

"Dalu", Mrs. Eugenia said. "Thank you Moses for your hospitality".

"No need to say more right now," he politely said motioning to the large audience at the table. He continued:

"Don't worry, Mrs. Eugenia we will discuss all this in private later. Now is the time to eat."

Mrs. Eugenia was grateful for this little respite, she waved at her nieces and nephews who sat at table and they waved back. "Good evening ma" they said in unison.

"Good evening children. I hope you are all doing well and studying hard. How was school today?"

"Yes ma." They responded in between mouthfuls, but they seemed more intent on eating at this time rather than discussing the progress of their studies.

Comfort sat down with Mrs. Eugenia by her side, and they served themselves of the steaming pot of egusi soup.

Everyone got one small piece of meat of the well cooked soup.

"Mmm, Comfort, this soup is nice today. I think if ever you decide you are tired of running a cloth shop you might want to try a restaurant business." Mrs. Eugenia said in all earnest.

Comfort laughed.

"Sister that is the last thing I want to do. Although, I do love cooking very much, but the thought of cooking day in and day out, I think would change my mind about it. Right now I cook for pleasure. I do catering on the side; I have started cooking for weddings and for big parties."

"You know I had no idea of that." Her sister answered.

"Well, it is not long since I started it with some friends of mine." She replied. "We do it on weekends when the market is slow, we contract out; and it is quite nice really because we go where the party is. We bring our big pots, and cook on firewood in the backyard. But I have never thought that it could be my full time occupation."

"I myself was hoping to start a cake business but I never got any customers you know, so that put an end to it. But I bake for pleasure too or if any of my friends are having a party I can provide a cake for the occasion." Mrs. Eugenia said, not altogether unselfishly; who knows, she thought, she might have to start contracting herself out to bake cakes to make ends meet.

At the end of the meal Comfort arose to put away the cups and plates which were to be washed in the back yard.

The children were put to bed on their sleeping mats, and Mrs. Eugenia herself who had been up the whole previous night fell asleep on her own mat before she could relate to Moses her plight.

Once all the lights were out muffled whisperings could be heard coming from the single bed in the room which was for the master and mistress of the house, as Comfort explained how her sister had left with all her load and that tomorrow she would be gone to the house of Mrs. Chijioke the widow.

The newly wed Henrietta and Christian:

The day that Mrs. Eugenia unceremoniously moved out of her
marital abode, without any further to do, Mr. Christian took the day
off from work, and drove directly to the school where Henrietta was
a teacher. Filled with excitement he could not contain himself, and
he called her out from the staff room to tell her the good news.
"She moved!" He exclaimed excitedly. And he took her by the arm
and brushed his hand over her pregnant belly.
"This very morning I woke up to find that she had packed all of her
things; this is the day that we have waited for..."
"I told you Christian a long time ago, to tell her to go; and I cannot
for the life of me believe that you never said this to her earlier."
Christian shrugged his shoulders in response.
"I thought that I would wait her out, but you can see we have waited
a long time."

To have described Henrietta as beautiful would have been an
understatement. She was above average height for a woman, and
she had long slim legs. Her face was oval and her eyes were large
and always lined with a thick black liner which she also used to
accentuate her eyebrows. From the side she could have passed for
an image of Cleopatra. She was fair skinned and her eyes were a
hazel color. Her hair which was a nice brown color was always
relaxed; and unlike many less fortunate than herself, her hair thrived
despite the harsh chemicals this entailed and was long and thick.
Needless to say, her beauty was obvious, and it was this that had
initially attracted Christian to her. However, it was in actuality her
ease of manner and lightheartedness which had robbed his soul. His
wife was all boring duty and business. For the most part she made
him feel unnerved and took everything so seriously with no time for
laughter. With Henrietta his soul felt free and at ease. It was only
after he had been with Henrietta that he had understood what love

really was; and he had felt like a fool for thinking that his feelings for his wife had once been love.

As for Henrietta, indeed, if not for her undying passion for Christian, she could probably have done very well for herself, and have married much earlier and much better. She was a romantic of sorts, and against her families' wishes, and even her own good sense, she had held onto Christian and the love they had for each other. She had consoled herself with the fact that after all a marriage certificate is just a paper, and here she had Christian in her arms every night. So what difference did it make if she had the marriage certificate or not? Moreover, since she had fears about her ability to conceive a child with her lover, she was even less likely to attempt to pursue another relationship. (There were many selfish reasons as well as unselfish ones keeping the relationship in check.) As such, with the advent of her much longed for pregnancy, it seemed that fate had finally given the relationship its blessings, or at least condoned it.

A traditional wedding in Onitsha:

Henrietta's family lived in Onitsha in a small bungalow in the G.R.A. Although they had lived in the town of Onitsha their whole lives, they were not really indigenes of Onitsha. The family actually hailed from Owerri. Due to the general insecurity in the east, it had been determined that the risks associated with a traditional wedding in Owerri were too high; and as such it was decided that the traditional ceremony should be much abbreviated and modified to be held in town.

The town of Owerri had been the epicenter of many kidnap dramas, and not wanting to tempt fate, the patriarch Mr. Henry Okeke had decided to hold the wedding in town. Mr. Henry Okeke was a wealthy trader in Onitsha, and had the means to secure the services of several armed guards who could be seen roaming the premises with their AK 47's ready. The security was tight, and the gate to the compound was kept closed. All the guests were rigorously checked against a guest list kept at the gate house before they could be admitted. Overall, Mr. Okeke was not displeased at the wedding; on the contrary he was much relieved that his eldest daughter from his first wife was finally going to get married at the ripe age of 34 years. Hypocritically enough he probably would have preferred for her to have been the only wife of Christian; but in this case he felt that as beggars, they could not really be choosers. The cause of their beggarliness was multifold; for the first part, Henrietta was in years far beyond the marrying age for most people in their circles. Secondly, her affair with Christian had been well publicized, all over Enugu and Onitsha, that no single man, even should he have found her desirable, would have dared to approach her. Moreover, to make matters worse, it was not as if the girl was socially out there meeting people; unless, of course, Christian was with her. In effect, she had been as a wife in all but name.

Mrs. Clementina Okeke, the first wife of Henry, and the mother of Henrietta, was busy on the occasion. She had arranged for the caterers, and was seeing to the arrangement of the chairs in the courtyard so as to allow the grooms family to sit on one side, and the bride's family to sit on the other. She was slightly out of sorts, as she had hoped for a white wedding; but it seemed as if that was not going to be a possibility, as the Anglican church had out rightly refused to wed a man, who was already married in church, to someone else. But, she too was no fool when it came to matters of practicality. It had taken sixteen years to bring Christian to the altar; although, in reality, it was no altar at all, but the courtyard of a bungalow in Onitsha. The mother remained mystified as to the attraction her daughter had for this man Christian, and she failed totally to see what her daughter found so irresistible in him. But, then they had long since learnt that Henrietta had a mind of her own, and any attempts on their part to dissuade her from the affair only served to reaffirm her love for him.
The outfits for the wedding had been carefully planned, and the color scheme had been diligently chosen to be a golden tone which so well complemented her daughters bronze skin. A red head tie was to

complement the out fit, and she had given her daughter a set of coral beads to wear on the occasion. Her pregnancy was still too early to show, and she still looked trim and fit in her wedding regalia. Christian was excited beyond words and sat in the front row with his people from Awka who were dressed in an Ankara of brown and green. In the presence of his mistress, soon to be wife, he was unrecognizable. He was gentle, considerate, and soft spoken. Gone were all the hints of irritation and the surly behavior he had so overtly displayed at home.

He could be heard laughing gently and talking calmly to his brother beside him, telling him about how relieved he was that Eugenia had finally got the message and left on her own accord.

His brother had laughed. "That woman!" He had said. "Mama always wondered how you could have married someone quite so boring."

Mrs. Christiana Nwafor sat with the women and had a smug look on her face. She was much relieved that her son had finally had the guts to leave the horrible wife Eugenia whom she could not stand at all.

After the formal introductions and the breaking of the cola nut, libations were poured to the spirits of the ancestors by pouring drink to the ground by the elder in the group from Mr. Henry Okeke's family.

Then the haggling for the bride price begun, which was done symbolically with the men carrying pieces of broom stick back and forth trying to set a monetary value on the bride. In the end the bride price was settled at a paltry sum of 10,000 Naira, and some goats and chickens and yams. The bride groom also promised that all the girls in the bride's home town would be sent little combs and mirrors and soap.

The time came for the handing over of the bride, and Henrietta was brought out and she was carrying in her right hand a cup of palm wine which she was to kneel down and offer the groom if she accepted his hand in marriage. So she came out with her cup and with her following of her cousins and friends. In her eyes could be seen a sparkling of happiness and on her lips lingered a soft smile as she strode out with the cup in her hand. but for all they looked they could not see Christian anywhere. A murmuring of anticipation went through the crowd, as she searched row after row for Christian. Nearly giving up, they finally spotted him as having intentionally hidden deep inside the crowd. The girls proceeded to where he was and she gave him to drink while kneeling down before him, and he drunk from the cup and then he stood up from his chair when she stood up, and in an uncharacteristic fashion he wowed the crowd by going down on his knee, something he was not supposed to do, and then he asked, out loud:

"My dear Henrietta, will you be mine forever?"

A hum of murmuring could be heard from the crowd.

Finally an old man from the Awka group came over and started trying to pull Christian to his feet.

"Get up, Ogene ne me Gi? What is wrong with you? Don't you know it is the woman who is supposed to kneel with the palm wine and for you to drink and not the other way?"

Christian refused to budge.

"Hapu makam. Obero new times, new ways? I want to publicly declare my love for my wife?"

"My friend don't be a total fool. Please get up and stop making a spectacle of your self." His friends came over and forced him up to his feet.

Nevertheless, this public display of his love became the talk of Enugu, and Onitsha and even Awka. Christian had inadvertently gone down in history as the first Igbo man who publicly prostrated for a woman at a wine carrying ceremony.

Mrs. Oby Chijioke returns from her annual trip to Lagos:

Mrs. Oby Chijioke had just returned from her annual trip to Lagos. She had barely finished her bucket bath when her maid was knocking on the door.

"Madam! Please can you come to the parlor and see Mrs. Eugenia right away as she says she has an urgent message for you."

Mrs. Oby Chijioke was alarmed. She quickly put on a Boo boo and went as quickly as she could to the parlor. On her arrival she found Mrs. Eugenia Nwafor seated in the Love seat. Her hair was disheveled from the preceding day's activities and she sat motionless with a dazed gaze looking into space, deep in thought.

Beside her stood her trunk, suitcase, and carboard box, as telltale signs of her fate.

Mrs. Oby Chijioke came in, and sensing that something must be very amiss she gently placed her hand on her friends shoulder before saying ever so softly.

"Tell me Mrs. Eugenia; is this all your load? What is the matter?"

"Christian has married Henrietta", was the simple reply given.

"I thought as much." Her friend answered, "Oh dear! I must admit that for long I had suspected that something like that might happen." Her friend continued.

"Yet, Mrs. Oby, you never said this to me or anything even close."

Mrs. Eugenia Nwafor burst into tears; a flood gate of tears poured down her cheeks, as all the emotions of the last few days finally overcame her.

" Ewo, Ewo me" Ka ngwa gi ! Chukwu na me, chukwu na me" She wailed.

"Why did this happen to me? When I walked down the aisle I was the happiest bride east of the River Niger! Then you know, I do not know or understand how or why this happened? But I can tell you for the last sixteen years we have lived under the shadow of Henrietta."

"Now tell me what exactly happened. Was it Christian who asked you to leave?"

"Actually no" She replied, not understanding the apparent relevance that everyone except herself placed upon this little detail. For all she knew, or cared, the effect was the same, and that was that she was now no longer in her marital home, and in all probablity never would be again.

Then she continued,

"I moved out without being asked to, when I found out that he had scheduled his traditional wedding to Henrietta."

Her friend's face lit up,

"How brave of you! I wish that all women could see this example of courage."

Her friend seemed surprised to hear this and asked shyly,

"Do you truly think it a courageous act to leave your husband, or are you just saying so for my sake? What about it makes it courageous?"

"I think it is the courage to stand up for the truth and for your beliefs. What beliefs? You may ask. The answer is Christianity, of course. And no matter how the men may want to tweak it, we repudiated polygamy with the advent of Christianity, no? Yet so many of our men pick and choose what pleases them from Christianity and our traditional beliefs. I think that is a sham."

Mrs. Eugenia Nwafor hears the reports second hand about the wedding:

The reports slowly filtered back through the grapevine to Enugu and even to Mrs. Eugenia Nwafor's ears, through the belligerent reports from her enemies. The rumor about town was that the wedding had been a spectacular success and that Christian had done the unthinkable act of kneeling down like an oaf before his mistress of sixteen years in public. He was alternately described as a desperado or as being deeply in love depending on who gave the reports. The women folk were secretly impressed by the scandal; all except Mrs. Eugenia herself who felt ashamed to acknowledge that this oaf was once her husband; and the only reason she thought of him as an oaf was because he could never have done this for her. However, the men were more scandalized thinking that this could lead to a near societal upheaval with the male superiority assured to tumble down. To say the least, the action of Christian's which had been on the spur of the moment was to prove to be near unprecedented in its scope.

The evening she heard of the wedding she had listened in disbelief that this cold fish she had been married to for so many years could muster up so much emotion and feelings for some one other than his real wife.

Mrs. Eugenia Nwafor breaks down:

It was not long after this, that one day Mrs. Eugenia Nwafor had confided in her friend Mrs. Oby Chijioke:

"Sometimes, I feel like I have descended into this dark tunnel, or depression if you will. It is a situation over which I am totally powerless. My heart is broken. I say to myself, 'even in this rejection I must find my salvation'. Like all trials sent by divine providence they are not ones of our own choosing; rather what God has seen fit to send us. Of all the sorrows in the world, this was one I would never have chosen. So here I am in this deep dark tunnel, and all I know is that I must stay down here as long as He chooses; and at His pleasure I will come out again. I try to be patient, and I try to be of good cheer; but the truth is that right now I can only be described as a most sordid and pathetic companion, and rightfully so. Indeed, there can hardly be a more wasteful exercise than to be impatient with God."

Mrs. Oby Chijioke could see the pain in her friends eyes and thoughtfully responded,

"It is amazing how painful rejection can be," she said, "And to make matters worse the heart does not discern which rejections merit feelings of sadness. It is one thing to be a child and rejected by your mother, and quite another to be spurned by an unfaithful husband. In

the former case, the sadness is justified, but in the latter case, the feeling should be a reflection of an injustice. I know what sadness I felt after the death of my husband; there were days where I did not want to move, so deep was my sorrow." Then she pensively added, as if an afterthought,
"But we all are here now seeking to find a way to understand the incomprehensible, to make sense of the meaning of life, and love and death." " Yes, we will always be left to wonder, why one man who perhaps loves life dies young, and another lives to old age hating every day of it…."

The days turned to weeks and right on time, before the children were to return home for the holidays, Mrs. Eugenia Nwafor was able, by luck, to secure a nice two bedroom apartment in New Haven. Her friend, Mrs. Oby Chijioke, was sorry to see her friend go, but understood fully the need for Mrs. Eugenia Nwafor to try to reestablish her independence and to stand on her own feet. It was not until her friend had left and Mrs. Oby Chijioke was sitting alone at dinner, that she realized how lonely she had been since the death of her husband two years earlier. Paul had succumbed to what had been attributed to have been an acute cardiac event, when he had suddenly slumped over the dining table after dinner. An ambulance had been called, but by the time the ambulance had arrived at the hospital there had been no life left in him. Mrs. Oby Chijioke had been shocked beyond belief.
It is one thing to be single and to have never married, and quite another to have been married, and then to suddenly find yourself a widow. There is no state in life for which people are more ill prepared than this state, as all who marry, only think of the happy end, "and then they lived happily ever after", and they forget the last part of the vow, the stipulation, " 'til death do us part". In this way the advent of death is always a surprise. (For the vow does not have power over life and death.)
"No", she thought to herself as she sat alone at her dining table, and the thunder was loud, and the rain poured down in a torrent, as if God himself were angry.

"We must seize what little joy there is that God allows us, and greedily hold this to our soul, for there is no guarantee of anymore. There is nothing more to life."

She wished that she and Paul had spent more time doing nice things; instead it was as if they had worried every day, about everything, up until the day that he died. The little joy that could have been gleaned out of the day was instead left to waste by the side.

"How I wish that I had known better", she said to herself, remembering the saying that was so often repeated by the priest at church, " the cup is either half full or half empty. and , "Which one are you going to choose today?" For it was a choice, a conscious choice, that had to be made everyday.

Nay, happiness was not so much a state, as a decision; to be happy, with how ever little or much the day had to offer, to be happy and to learn to turn the little sorrows into joys. It was her own little attempt to "light the candle and not to curse the darkness".

Yet even in spite of all these gentle and noble thoughts her heart was often heavy with the sorrow of loss. Even though it was two years since he had passed, each time she remembered, it was like a sword going through her heart. How many mornings had she not awoken thinking he was beside her still? Only for the daylight to prove her wrong. In her dreams, he was still alive, and now and then he would come to her in her dreams, and it would seem as if he had never died. Yes, Mrs. Oby Chijioke was a Christian, and she believed in life after death, and it was this consolation alone which kept her going. But, in her heart, she felt cheated by fate. She had married for companionship, and now this companionship fate had snatched right from her hands, unexpectedly and violently in complete disregard of her need. In futility, her mind would try to unwind the events of that fateful day, so as to suspend them in time, and to stop forever what had happened. She would replay the events over and over again, trying to no avail to stop what had already transpired.

Mrs. Eugenia Nwafor the divorcee:

The town of Enugu, the 'crown jewel' of the pre- civil war era Eastern Region of Nigeria is a city located less than an hour by car east of the famous River Niger. The city was originally constructed by the British colonialists in the Southern Protectorate of the Niger, when coal was discovered. In it's colonial hey day, it was a city of two worlds which rarely if ever met; on the one hand, there was the Coal Camp area of the town which was where the natives who worked the coal camps lived with their families. And on the other hand on the other side of town, there was the Government reserved area. This G.R.A was reserved for the colonial masters, and indeed, if any native ventured into this area without cause, it was punishable by a beating at the very least and possibly even a prison sentence for trespassing. The majority of the Europeans had left after Nigerian independence; and whatever remnant, evacuated with the civil war. The newer areas within the city , middle class areas such as New Haven, lying adjacent to the Independence Layout and Uwani on the other side of the town are perfectly respectable middle class areas of the town, though of medium density. The Independence Layout which was initially sparsely developed with just a few ministerial homes, but had since become more congested, though not overly so, with a multitude of houses and apartment like dwellings. The Government house, was the prize of the Independence Layout, and w it's large imperious gates were guarded and closed to the public at large. In the forefront of the government house there was an area of land which had become converted into a park, with grass planted and trees, and flowers and this was open to the public and named Michael Okpara square.

For the most part Enugu had started out as a boring civil servant town, in direct contradistinction to the metropolis of Onitsha which laying beside the River Niger had been the economic capital of the East, and this economic activity pre dated colonialism. In the center of town there is a high density area called Asata which exists on the slope of a hill leading down to a small stream which transects the city,and whose tributary runs adjacent to the major Ogbete market. and this area has mostly unplanned buildings. Some of the buildings are squalid, though even here most are of decent construction.

On the other side of the University Campus, the Kenyatta Market is surrounded by the township of Uwani, and further west and south of this is Awkunaw, and Agbani. The Udi hills frame the city to the west and the hills immediately adjacent to the city are named for a British settler, Milliken, and retain that name to this day. Like many cities in the third world the town of Enugu had experienced a unprecedented population explosion over the past twenty years with masses of young rural inhabitants of the surrounding regions migrating to the towns in search of work. This was mostly futile as there was no work to be found in the towns, and indeed the urban migrants would have most probably been better off farming in the villages, but this was not their preference.

The flat in New Haven had been secured at the last minute right before the children were to return home for the Easter Holidays. The flat was on Chime Avenue, and was on the third floor of a nice building with secure high walls and a gate man. Although it was only a two bed room flat ,she was excited to have her independence back. Nevertheless, although outwardly, on the surface at least, everything had the appearance of normalcy, the truth was that for Mrs. Eugenia this all felt most unusual. She had never lived on her own before, having gone straight from her father's home into her marital home; and now she had been forced to see a different side of a world that she knew little of.

To make matters worse, there were the constant fears and insecurities that besiege all single women, that she now had to contend with. The fact was that Chinedu was now the man of the house, a mere boy of the age of eighteen.

Mrs. Eugenia Nwafor had to furnish the little flat, and she also had to put on some kind of face for her children, so that they would not be aware that her heart was really broken. She felt that there was no need for her to plague them with her sorrows. In any case, there was little she could say, that would be proper in the present circumstances. For no matter what she would say, it would be hard to say anything positive about Christian to the children; yet it would be in poor taste to castigate him publicly while the children were there. As such, she had decided upon the wisdom of silence on the matter of Christian and Henrietta as far as the children were concerned.

Mrs. Eugenia Nwafor at work:

The offices of the Department of Agriculture of Enugu state were located in the main offices of the state government. This was on a side road, adjacent to Park lane, in G.R.A. Enugu.
 Mrs. Eugenia Nwafor had been most fortunate in securing her position. She had been a complete unknown, and a newly wed, when the partition of the old East Central State government had taken place; first, into Anambra and Imo states; and then, a few years later , Anambra state had been subdivided into Enugu state and Anambra state. Likewise, Imo state had been divided into Imo and Abia states. With the new partition having taken place; all indigenes that "hailed from Anambra state", had been relieved of their duties and forced to seek employment at Awka, the new capital of Anambra State. Although, Christian hailed from Awka, his wife was an indigene of Udi; and as such, she was able to use this fact to seek for employment with the Enugu State Government. Many positions had been open, and she had gladly taken up her position as head secretary and administrative assistant to the Permanent Secretary of the Department of Agriculture, Mr. Emmanuel Udeh. The process of gaining employment could not have been easier; all she had to do was to prove her hometown was in Enugu State, and that she had a degree from an institution of higher learning, and the job had been hers.
 She had studied and completed a course in business management at the Institute of Management and Technology in Enugu. Whilst a

student at IMT, she had met her future husband, Christian Nwafor. Engineer Christian Nwafor hailed from the town of Awka, in the present day Anambra state. Christian had been introduced to her by her cousin, John Onuorah, who had been a class mate of his, at the University of Nigeria Nsukka, where they had both been studying civil engineering.

Christian had been quite infatuated with her at the time, and had boasted to his family that Eugenia had an education, and that her hips were designed for 'childbearing'.

The courtship had progressed rapidly. On certain weekends, when he could spare the time, he would arrive in Enugu for the weekend by taxi. And they would spend the weekend going to parties held at the Student's union at Enugu campus. Or, go to a night club to dance for the evening. Over a period of four months they had dated. Then Christian had proposed. He had never really dated any lady seriously before, and being a 'religious man', he could not anticipate staying in a dating relationship for an extended period of time without marriage. Mrs. Eugenia Nwafor's family had been overjoyed at the occasion of his proposal. Their oldest daughter had graduated from IMT, and barely six months after her graduation was to wed. Soon after her wedding, she had been most fortunate as to gain employment at the Department of Agriculture of Enugu State; and she had held onto this job, through all the ups and downs of her marriage, and in the process she had outlived a succession of ministers, and permanent secretaries in her post.

Initially, out of shame over her condition ,she had said nothing about her divorce at work. Her co workers had ,however, heard through the grape vine about the wine carrying ceremony that had taken place at Onitsha. No one had dared to say anything about the second wife. Judging from her sadness they had found it easy to conjecture that what ever Christian had done, it had not been entirely with his wife's blessing.

To further pique their curiosity Mrs. Oby Chijioke had come to pick her from work on several occasions. On one of those occasions she had let it slip out that they were going home for supper; that the young ladies of the office were now certain that Mrs. Eugenia was in the middle of a 'dreadful divorce'.

"Eya," Ijeoma the junior secretary said to her friend Mrs. Janet Nwosu .

"I told you I was certain that she had left her husband. I told you I was sure two weeks ago when she came and went in the same dress two days in a row and her step was heavy."

Mrs. Janet Nwosu who was a lady of the world was not too impressed.

"It is not the end of the world. But what can she do, after nineteen years of marriage? To get up and leave? Surely that must be a sign of madness. If it is me, I no go go. Go for what? When you leave you just are making it easier for the new wife."

Ijeoma laughed.

"I think it is better to avoid this type of situation self. Do not let your husband stray, for you can find it hard to regain lost ground."

Mrs. Janet Nwosu who was several years older than Ijeoma shrugged her shoulders.

"All you young girls, who have never married, are always full of advice. I don't think any wife ever assisted her husband to stray. I think the question is how do you stop him from straying? If there was a way to do this, I know Mrs. Eugenia personally, and I guarantee you, she would have found the way if this thing existed."

Ijeoma smiled, "never mind me Mrs. Janet, I am always full of ideas and always looking for answers."

The news spread through the department like wildfire. It was whispered as she walked by, by all, from the messengers to the minister himself. As she walked by, in hushed voices they would say. " ne gu de ya," " Yes, that is the one who left her husband after nineteen years of marriage."

Some pitied her, but by far the majority thought that the news was laughable and they sniggered behind her back. To the men she was an example of a fallen woman; a woman who with education had become too big for her britches. She was a woman who thought she was a man and had left her husband. After all was not polygamy as natural as life itself; it was in our blood, it was our blood, it was our culture, Christianity or no Christianity. Or it was a ready excuse for society to fall back on to excuse the shortcomings of the men.

Home for the holidays:

Easter had come and the children were on holiday from their respective boarding schools.. Mr. Christian and Henrietta had traveled to Calabar to visit the sister of Henrietta; and the children Henrietta, Chinedu, Afam, and Christiana were at the home of their mother on Chime Avenue. Mrs. Eugenia Nwafor had taken vacation from the offices of the Department of Agriculture, and was resting at home with her children. The days went by quickly. During the day they would take care of various chores, and then in the evening they would all try, as best they could, to amuse themselves by reading, or playing board games. There was no chance to use the television sitting in the corner because there was never electricity in the evening. The ceiling fans were of no use, and the heat was becoming oppressive. The children were not amused by the absence of a generator. At school there was a generator which provided two hours of precious electricity in the night; enough to allow the students to do their prep with light. Here they had to read and do everything by kerosene light.

The apartment at Uwani had been locked up for the week, and there was no chance for them to visit there, even during the day, and get some respite from the heat. Mrs. Eugenia could not even store food in a refrigerator and as such each morning they would cook fresh food, and any food left over from the previous dinner would have to be re heated meticulously, to prevent it from spoiling..

Miriam the maid was busy having to do daily shopping at the market AND THEN COOKING FOR THE FAMILY.

Mrs. Eugenia enjoyed the company, she did not really mind the hustle and the bustle, and for this was what she lived for.

"Mother, tell me how do you survive in this place, with neither light nor water?" the oldest boy had asked his mother after observing her suffering.

"I survive because I have to." She had replied, "My dear, when I grew up we had no light at all, and we had no refrigerator in the village, and we survived very well. It is only when you are used to light and they take it from you that it becomes hard to stand the heat and,.."

" Well, in our school we have two hours of light every evening; and I try to do everything during those hours, to have my bath, brush my teeth and then study, and then we go to bed early because we are not allowed to be up with live candle light. Oh, and God forbid you have to use the bathroom, and then you need a flash light to find your way. It is amazing."

"Two hours of light what a blessing! I would do anything to have two hours of light. I don't even know when the last time I watched the television here. It is a cruel joke, to own a television and also to have a refrigerator! Never mind, my dears, Miriam has covered for all this by buying food in small quantities and cooking every day; we will get by. Sometimes, I remember the big deep freeze we had in Uwani, and what a luxury that was. I also remember sitting in the cool of the air con in the living room and saying to myself that I needed a sweater. Those days are long gone. Here I sometimes will have three showers a night to cool off. One day in March I poured water on the cement floor to see if by allowing it to evaporate I could cool the room down. I think the heat is getting worse, but I think I will get used to it. Over the summer we will go to Lagos and stay with Aunt Margaret and she has a generator and an air conditioner which is on every night."

'Ah, mom, I look forward to that. Lagos is always interesting. We will be able to watch movies on the video player as well, that will be a nice holiday"

"Well if your father releases you, like he did this time."

 "Don't worry, mom, I think Henrietta is getting more tired of us by the day, and she has been on bed rest for the past two weeks. That was why they left town to go to her sister's house for her to rest."

"I wonder how she can be overworked. It is quite amazing. What does she do any way? It is not as if she holds down a job of any sort, because she stopped working the day she married your father."

'She is busy keeping house. Donatus left after you left, he was too upset to stay with the new madam and he kept comparing you with her that it quite distressed dad and Henrietta and they had to let him go."

"Oh, my dear faithful Donatus, I miss him so; but I could never have afforded his salary now on my meager income. I know he will do well for himself. He told me he was saving to start a business for himself and that should be a good thing."

Mrs. Margaret Obiora comes to Enugu on a visit:

Mrs. Margaret Obiora was the second daughter of Mr. and Mrs. Samuel Okafor. She was two years younger than her older sister Mrs. Eugenia Nwafor and two years older than the youngest girl Comfort. Of all the sisters, Eugenia and Margaret were the closest and they had each other's confidences. She had received a telephone call from Mrs. Eugenia relating how she had moved out four month's earlier; and at the nearest opportunity she had purchased a bus ticket from Lagos to Enugu to check on her sister.

Mrs. Margaret Obiora was the wife of a successful trader by the name of Mr. Charles Obiora. To his friends and business associates he was fondly known as 'Charlie'. He had a stall in Onitsha main market, and one in Lagos Island from which he sold Motor spare parts. His younger brother Oke ran the Onitsha market end of the business, and he took care of the Lagos end of the business. A considerable amount of his time was spent in Apapa trying to clear his goods through the customs. He had the assistance of several young men from his home town who were employed in the shop and ran it for him while he was away on business. The family rented a nice flat in Ikeja.

The fact that 'business had been good lately', could be seen on the wrapper that graced the slim waist of Mrs. Margaret Obiora; and the bright yellow hue of the head tie which graced her beautifully coiffured hair, only served to reaffirm this fact.. In all things external she was the opposite of her sister Mrs. Eugenia. Whereas Mrs. Eugenia was stout, and rather short and dark; her sister Margaret was tall, and yellow, and slim. She walked gracefully with her spine ram rod straight; as if she had been brought up in the village balancing water bottles on her head. In terms of her wealth, she was the opposite of the sister Comfort. She was educated to the level of the National certificate of education. As her husband was so wealthy, she did not deem it necessary to work; and instead she stayed at home and toyed with various projects, sometimes attempting a shop, or a business which never took off. In the end she had given up on being a business woman, and had resigned herself to fate, to just being a home maker. Her five children were away at boarding school, and she had a period of one week to stay in Enugu whilst her husband was away in Cotonou on business.

From the motor park where the luxury bus discharged it's passengers at 5pm, she was able to secure a taxi to take her to her sister's new address on Chime Avenue in New Haven. It was the middle of April, and the rains had not started yet; and everywhere was still brown, and dry, and dusty. There was the smell of burning grass always in the air; and over the horizon could be seen smoke rising up in the sky as the farmers set their traditional fires to clear the forest, and burn the bush.

The taxi let her off in the front of the store. Not knowing the way into the building she asked a question of the store keeper, who knew Mrs. Eugenia, and directed her to the back of the compound through the gate, and past the gate man to the stairwell which led up the three flights of stairs to Mrs. Eugenia's new flat. At the top of the stairs she knocked on the door. The new maid Miriam answered the door, and let her in, on ascertaining that this was Mrs. Eugenia's sister. She sat down in the living room and waited eagerly for the arrival of her sister. As she sat she looked around the little living room which had now become furnished to a certain extent. There were some easy chairs arranged in a circle with a center small table. Off to the side the little television sat on a cardboard box. There was a small café style dining table with four chairs where the meals were served. Mrs. Eugenia had even managed to put some curtains in the living room. The ceiling fan sat stationary in the ceiling above..

At a little after five thirty p.m. Mrs. Eugenia Nwafor arrived home accompanied by her friend the widow Mrs. Oby Chijioke. The sisters hugged each other and Margaret hugged Mrs. Oby Chijioke as well.

"Long time" They said to each other.

"Well, you look well." Margaret said, she had feared the worst for her sister.

Mrs.Oby Chijioke smiled.

"You know now she looks fine, but I can tell you six months ago she was not quite herself. She was exhausted and it was difficult." Margaret nodded her head.

"I can imagine. I came as soon as I could. It has been one thing after the other; the children have been home or on their way to school, and Charlie would not release me until he went on this trip to Cotonou, and I insisted that as he was going to be gone there was no need for me to stay and looking at the walls."

Mrs. Eugenia smiled.

"You look well Margaret. What is this you are wearing? Is this the latest wrapper from Lagos?"

"I don't know Oh. I found it at the shop where I buy my cloth, and I thought, well I will try it out. "

"Now give me all the gossip from Lagos. What is the latest there?"

"I am hardly the one to keep abreast of all these things. Lagos will always be Lagos. There vanity has found a happy home."

The ladies laughed.

"Vanity and ostentation are the watch words of Lagos." Mrs. Chijioke replied as she herself, knew Lagos very well.

"You must make an effort to stay out of the competition because you can easily get caught up trying to keep up with the Jones's there."

Mrs. Margaret opened up her suitcase and gave her sister a gift of white lace.

"I bought this for you, thinking you might be able to sew a up and down for your self to cheer your self up. And here is a head tie I bought for you in sky blue material."

"I don't need this "Mrs. Eugenia protested.

Mrs. Chijioke insisted.

"Of course, Mrs. Eugenia, you must take this. Is it because you don't have a husband that you will no longer wear nice clothes? Then you will truly look like an object of pity to the entire world. No my dear, you may be the rejected one. It is alright, but you will hold your head up high once again, and say 'that even in this rejection I shall find my salvation'"

Mrs. Margaret seemed to agree.

"Sister Eugenia, you need to come to Lagos and see for your self. In Lagos, half of all the women have never married at all, and the other one quarter are the second or third wife of some body or the other. And they are all holding their heads up high, and not hiding their heads in shame. In Lagos it is the divorced women who are the happy ones'."

Mrs. Eugenia looked at her sister in disbelief.

"Here in the east it is like a taboo. When I come in to the office, they all stop talking. And when I walk past an Office, I can hear them asking, Is that the one who got divorce?"

"In fact the other day, Henrietta sent me a letter, as she was worried that she may have difficulty getting married in the future having come from a divorced home."

Mrs Margaret Obiora continued:

"That is why I am so happy I have had the fortune of living in Lagos. Truly it has expanded my horizon, and has taught me a compassion for the human condition far removed from the narrow mindedness of the east. That is not to say that I do not praise the institution of Marriage, nor to say that I am not appreciative of it. No, but I think the problem is when we want to be married just for the sake of saying that we are married. We continue in these unions only too often when they should have been repudiated out rightly in instances of physical abuse or mental cruelty. Then we have lost sight of the goal of marriage, and are in it only for the sake of being married".

"It is a weakness of our women this urge to be married." Said Mrs. Chijioke with much introspection.

 Mrs. Margaret Obiora agreed,

 "I think you have put it right, a weakness in our women … and to make matters worse it seems as if there is no amount of education which will dispel this notion from their minds. Ah, our women are bound to their husbands for generations to come."

Mrs. Chijioke nodded in agreement.

"There is nothing wrong in and of itself to be bound to one's husband, Margaret. If I must say so, I was very happily bound to My Paul, who treated me so nicely, may his soul rest in peace. Where I have a problem with this is where the husband takes upon himself the role of an abuser either physically or mentally, there we must use our reason and unbind the relationship."

Mrs. Eugenia looked up at this point.

"Thank you Mrs. Chijioke, I feel redeemed now."

"Of course you are redeemed my dearest, you who suffered so at the hands of Christian and for so long."

Mrs. Margaret agreed, "You, my dear sister, are a saint. Only a saint could have stayed on with such patience. And mark my words, your children may not now understand the great sacrifice you made for them on their behalf, but one day I think they will. But, as I was saying in Lagos, this is the usual state of affairs. I worry much myself, what will happen if Charlie continues to do so well with his business? Will he decide he needs another wife too, and maybe he will find one in Onitsha on one of his trips there. For all I know he could have one there already and I am the only one who does not know!"

The ladies laughed.

"Margaret, I do not think that Charlie would do that." Mrs. Eugenia Nwafor responded with all seriousness.

"You say this with such confidence that I myself could not use. I will not vouch for anyone but myself. I must confess that even Charlie has had his short comings that I have found out about."

"But never of the magnitude or the duration of Christian and Henrietta."

"The children tell me Henrietta is due in July, and that she has prepared a room and a crib. John says that their father is talking continuously about the baby. I found that slightly disconcerting because I remember when I was expecting he never even discussed one thing with me. And he never assisted in the up bringing of the children; it sounds now like it is the opposite."

"I told you before to not discuss the goings on at their father's house. It serves no purpose other than to stir up your emotions. Time will tell."

Margaret was happy to be back in the East. She enjoyed Lagos for all the amenities it had to offer, but she found that sometimes the traffic was tiring and the hustle and the bustle was a little more than she cared for. The children had all been sent to attend school in the east, and over the next two days she prepared to go on a visit to the schools as well. She went to the little store below Mrs. Eugenia's house and bought cabin biscuits and dried milk and cornflakes and squash. The provisions were equally divided into three boxes. During the day she stayed indoors and waited for Mrs. Eugenia to return from work, and then she would keep her sister company at dinner, and they would chat about the good old days when papa and mama were still alive. These conversations usually took place after dinner when they used a small kerosene lamp that stood on the dining table to light up the room. For the past three months there had not been more than one hour of electricity per night in the eastern part of the country. Mrs. Eugenia had been spoiled at her husband's flat by the use of a generator. Over here in New Haven she had to manage with candle light and the kerosene lamp.

As night fell they could hear the firing of gun shots in the distance, as the armed robbers were battling with the police in town. It seemed as if every night the gun battles grew fiercer and were often quite close. When night fell the big Iron Gate was closed across the door which led into the apartment, and all the windows were closed. They said their prayers together, for it was only God who could safe guard them.

Only too soon had the week passed by and it was time for the two sisters to part and say good bye. Mrs. Margaret Obiora had to return to Lagos to meet her husband Charlie who was expected back that night from Cotonou. The three children had been visited at the Ambassador College in Agbani and all the provisions delivered. Mrs. Chijioke had kindly agreed to transport Mrs. Obiora early on Friday morning to the premises of the luxury bus compound that served the Lagos Enugu route. Mrs. Eugenia Nwafor had risen earlier than usual and had prepared a nice breakfast of bacon and eggs for her sister. She had packed a small container of rice and stew for her to have as a lunch on her way and there was a cold bottle of iced water for the journey. At the bus stop she had bought her ticket and taken her place and kissed her sister goodbye.
"Come again soon Margaret"
But Margaret was more intent on having Mrs. Eugenia come to Lagos.
"No you must come next time, and stay with me."

Charity meeting;

'Mrs. Eugenia, I'm here waiting for you, I've been waiting for the last thirty minutes where you are?"

"I am still at work, Oh dear! I had completely forgotten about the meeting. I will leave here directly and should be at home by 5.00 pm. Please get started without me.'

Mrs. Eugenia Nwafor stood up from the chair that sat behind her desk. The papers she had been working upon were strewn across her desk. She placed them in a brown file and placed the file in her desk drawer.

No one was left in the office of the Department of Agriculture. She closed the door to the office behind her and carrying her hand bag in one hand and a small plastic bag containing some fruits she had bought during her lunch hour she walked out on the street. Where she flagged down an Okada driver to take her to New Haven.

In the distance the Millikent hills towered majestically over the city and with the sun beginning to set in the west the rays of the sun were hitting the trees at an oblique angle and their shadows were long extending across the roadway. The Okada driver darted in and out between the cars and the buses. Mrs. Eugenia was always terrified of these journeys, sitting without a helmet at the back of the operator of the vehicle. She held on to him for dear life. The motorcyclist pulled up in front of the ground floor store that was the front of her building. He was given his fare.

The store keeper was sitting in a chair outside the door of the shop. "Good evening, ma. You are welcome". He greeted her.

Mrs. Eugenia set the plastic bag containing her fruits down on the ground for a moment whilst she retied her wrapper. Looking up she smiled and acknowledged the store keeper. "Kedu, You do well oh." After this brief exchange she hurried up the stairs to her flat where the meeting had started.

Christian women's association of New Haven:

Mrs Chijioke had spearheaded the initiative to start an organization to assist in the welfare of the increasing numbers of AIDs orphans. The plan had been to form a coalition of women who would seek to raise funds for the purchase of antiviral drugs, and also small donations to the local orphanages. Today was to be the first of a series of quarterly meetings. Invitations had been sent out to twelve close friends, but only two of their friends, Mrs. Nwakego and Mrs. Ebere had come. Mrs. Chijioke sat at the head of the café style dining table and was waiting for Mrs. Eugenia to come in order to start the meeting.

Mrs. Eugenia rushed in and greeted each of her friends with a hug. "You are all welcome"
She excused herself and disappeared to freshen up and then sat down opposite Mrs. Chijioke.
"Thank you all for coming." Mrs. Chijioke said." I had invited twelve ladies to join our association. Well, there are four of us here and I must say that I am delighted to have you all here. As we are so few, I want us to go ahead immediately with the election of officers. Mrs. Eugenia, I would like you to be responsible for keeping all the minutes Mrs. Nwakego, you will be the treasurer and Mrs. Ebere could you be the social secretary?"
"What would the duties of social secretary entail? " Mrs. Ebere asked.
"Well, if we do fund raising during a social event you would coordinate the activities>"
"I've never done anything quite like that before, "Mrs. Ebere answered dismayed.
"Oh not to worry." Mrs. Chijioke reassured her" We will not be involved in a lot of social activities. However we must do fund raising and I hope that as time goes on, and we identify different projects we would like to be involved with we can identify the cost and then seek ways to raise the money."
I have identified a number of orphanages who could do with our help. To start with I would like to make a site visit to one of the orphanages. We can make a small donation at the time. The real objective will be to see what they are most in dire need of".
"I would like us to start by donating half a bag of rice to St. Mary's orphanage in Transekulu. That will mean us raising ten thousand naira to purchase the bag of rice. Does anyone have any suggestions about how we can raise the funds?"
Mrs. Chijioke looked up from the paper where she was taking notes. "I cannot afford to donate money like that as my husband is deceased."

Mrs. Ebere suggested that they should sell lottery tickets for twenty naira a piece and that three months from the day they could pool the proceeds towards the bag of rice for the orphanage.

Regina comes to stay:

The lecturers of the higher institutions of learning had been on strike for nearly four months hoping to convince the government to increase the salaries of the lecturers to be en par with the salaries of the civil servants.
 Regina had been at home in Asata with her family for the time and was quickly growing tired of the over crowded conditions at her family home. When her cousins had returned to secondary school, she asked her aunt Mrs. Eugenia if it would be alright for her to stay for a while with her aunt so that she could study in peace away from her younger brothers and sisters. Mrs. Eugenia being only too happy to have some relief from the boredom of living alone, and happy to further the education of Regina in anyway she could was very happy to allow her to cone and stay in the other bedroom. During the day Regina would help Miriam the maid to cook and sometimes would do the marketing. Then she would sit down at the little café style dining table and try to study for her final exams which she would take whenever the university would resume. During the afternoons her friend from the school a young man by the name of Michael would come and spend some time with her, Michael was a year older than Regina. He was of average height with well proportioned limbs. His face was long and handsome. His eyes were lively and he was a charming conversationist who was studying agriculture at the Institute beside the commercial college Regina attended in Awka. He had ideas of opening a commercial farm, and having livestock. He talked excitedly about the advent of mechanized farming and irrigation methods. He was brimming with ideas about increasing productivity and taking the population into a new era where the man could live once again in proximity with the land and hope for success. He had dreams of ebbing the tide of rural dwellers and fortune seekers who came into the towns with high hopes of an easier life which the society could not provide.

Mrs. Eugenia sat and listened with amazement at the enthusiasm of the young man, all the more so since even after having worked for the offices of the permanent secretary of the department of agriculture for the past twenty years she had never heard any ideas so clearly expounded nor seen any project which could even have come close to his ambitions.

He was insistent. "Mrs. Eugenia I really see the future coming to crystallize into reality soon. We must increase the productivity of the farmers. We have the technology and the know how, and now we must seek for ways to develop this. I see the future unfolding in the rural arena and not in the putrid cities that lack all amenities. I cannot for the life of me understand why anyone would come, for instance and live in Enugu, where there is no work. The cost of living is expensive, and there are no amenities as water or electricity. One may as well stay in the village. But then that is how I think. I was brought up in my father's village, as he was retired by the time I was born. He taught me the fundamentals of farming in the traditional way and we still kept our farms and on holidays we would go and help our cousins with the farm. This was what sparked my interest in agriculture first and then secondly in rural life. I came to appreciate the nuances of village life which could be lost by the casual observer or the town dweller that only spent rare visits at home. It was a sleepy place, compared to the night clubs of town. For the villagers it was a hard life. You wake up early to walk a mile to fetch the water for the day, and then you go to the farm and you farm until the evening".

Mrs. Eugenia was most charmed by the young man, and soon came to look forward to his visits nearly as much as his fiancée.

"I am so pleased that you have met a man as sensible and talented as Michael," she had confided in Regina one evening after he had just left. "What does your father think of him?"

Regina had initially not answered the question then later she confessed that her father had in fact never met the young man, and that her father was more intent on her marrying a man by the name of Chief Obi.

"Auntie, I have never met Chief Obi, and I am worried about the way my father is pushing his suit for him. "

"If you have not met him, then how can your father be encouraging his suit?"

" Well, auntie, for the past one year, he and I have been communicating by letter, which is not a bad thing, although I think it is hard to really get to know anyone by letter alone. In a way it is quite frightening, for although you may think you are in love with the man of the letters, you don't really know until you meet him, as someone may appear very different in writing than in real life, and that is my main fear."

"At least you must have seen a picture of your friend?"

"Auntie, no and I was told that he is a divorcee and twenty years my senior."

Mrs. Eugenia was visibly perturbed by the information. "Now that is what I call outrageous, your father wants you to marry a divorcee, and as if that wasn't bad enough, the man is twenty years your senior!"

This outburst of Mrs. Eugenia's came out spontaneously, for a moment in her excitement she had forgotten that she herself belonged to that unmentionable category of people.

"Auntie!" Regina exclaimed.

"I know, you will say, but auntie you your self are divorced and I will tell you, but at least I am not pursuing a man in the hopes of remarriage."

"Well auntie, he told me this was a marriage for green card only." She continued.

"I have appealed to my father and to my mother many times. They have insisted that as a duty to my younger brothers and sisters I must marry well."

"So, for the sake of the family you will have to follow the sensible way, and not the way of the heart."

"My mother has said that love will surely follow quickly enough. And we have prayed and asked God for counsel, auntie, but God does not tell me what to do. Sometimes I think He says nothing because he wants me to follow my heart. But then there is no saying how many years it would take Michael to stabilize his situation, and without any inheritance of his own, where will he get funding to make all the big dreams materialize? I can see him, twenty years from now another embittered man whose life has no meaning with shattered dreams and bereft of hope. I think the question is, can I afford to marry a man who is as of now still an unknown entity, or should I, as my father says cast my lots with a man of some success."

As the story went on, the attraction to Chief Obi was further elaborated on as based upon his possession of a green card. It was this card that would enable Regina to go abroad and hopefully to send for her mother and father at a later date.

Mrs. Eugenia was surprised to hear all this. For some reason she had always assumed that Comfort would always be referred to as "Poor Comfort". Here she was receiving news that clearly demonstrated that Comfort and her husband had been hatching a plan for quite a long while that was to rescue them from their plight. It was no coincidence that Chief Obi lived abroad. The fact that they were Catholics, and that Regina had no business trying to marry a protestant who was even a divorced protestant had become immaterial. The family's condition was so poor that such little nuances of life had to be glossed over, and differences ignored so as to allow for the greater good of the family. In all this Regina seemed resigned to fate. The desperation of her family's home condition was no secret from her. One thing she had allowed herself, for the time being, for however brief the time might be she would indulge herself by allowing herself to enjoy the company of the young Michael. Sometimes, in the secret recesses of her heart she allowed herself to be in love with him. So great was her self discipline that even in her dreams she could not see herself married to this charming young man who did not have, and indeed could never acquire her father's blessing's.

Chief Obi:

Chief Obi was an Igbo man who had left home at the tender age of eighteen years to pursue a higher education in America. Whilst pursuing a Bachelors degree in Biology, and later a masters and PhD in the same subject, he had fallen in love with a beautiful American girl at the college. As fate would have it, Alice Rivers had fallen in love with him too. The two had had a whirlwind courtship and romance, and three children had dutifully followed in succession. Alice had even been taken back to Enugu to meet with Chief Obi's parents. When the last child had been sent away to college, Alice and Chief Obi decided to no longer hide their differences. Alice had moved out from the marital home on impulse, only to find that Chief Obi had cheerfully proceeded to start dating. (Although, there were rumors that the dating activities of Chief Obi preceded his wife's move.)

In any case, he had a quick succession of affairs, some with fellow Africans, and some with Americans. But none had proved to be a lasting affair, and that was when Chief Obi decided that the best way to proceed was to bring a young unspoiled girl from home. He dreamt of having a young girl beside himself again, and of being the envy of all his old friends with their old wives. In his mind he could imagine smells of egusi soup and okro soup emanating from the kitchen of his home. He could already hear himself whispering words of love in Igbo to his future wife, and her responding in Igbo. After having been away from the country of his birth for the better part of the last twenty years, everything about home had taken on an exaggerated importance. Forgotten were all the shortcomings of his home town and the annoying predilections of his own people.

In the letters he had received from Regina, he placed great hope. Unbeknown to her, Comfort had already mailed the fiancé a picture of Regina. Chief Obi had obediently sent back a picture of himself. The picture demonstrated clearly that he was an old man who was sadly out of shape, and suffering form the common western malaise of obesity. His pants were neatly belted under a pot belly. Comfort had on receiving the picture decided that the better course of action was to hide the picture, as she was certain that her daughter would reject the man outright if she knew what he looked like. This hiding the picture was in an effort to allow the relationship to proceed to a point of emotional involvement and no return from where Regina could not turn back. In the home in Asata the atmosphere had abruptly changed from one of unparalleled despair and constantly living on the precipice of despair, to a life of many potentialities, some real and some imagined. Chief Obi had become part of the every day banter of the household. EVEN THE YOUNGEST OF THE CHILDREN WAS well aware of this important man who they were yet to meet yet whose spirit hovered over their home as a benevolent benefactor waiting to unleash his opulence and wealth on them, to transform their poverty into a life of relative ease. At the end of the night prayers Comfort would add a prayer for the soon to be son in-law. "Thank you, Lord Jesus, for bringing us help in the form of an angel: Chief Obi."

In this way, it was possible to forget his condition; after all, he was an emissary of God, although in the form of a fat, divorced mortal.

The engagement party is arranged by the Chief:

A new hotel by the name of Hotel de Paris had just opened up. Chief Obi on arriving from the United states had been quite excited, and even before he had met his bride to be the first thing he had done was to go and inspect the premises of the proposed hotel. It was not by any means ostentatious, there was no swimming pool in the hotel, but then he intended to have an engagement party there, and not to swim, he thought to himself. There was a private room that could be rented for the night, there was space for twenty sundry tables and a small bar was situated off to the side of the room. A small stage was off to a corner, and would be suitable for a small band or a deejay to place his equipment for the evening. The two cousins walked around the room being led by the day time manager.

"You know chief, I don't think there is any need to hire a band, is that not just a waste of money? Why can't we use the hotel's deejay for the occasion?"

Chief Obi was not pleased, "Ahh aah, which one you dey now? I have come all the way from the U.S to have an engagement party; let us enjoy, small, before we go back to the land of the onye ocha."

Uche was not convinced, "I know, I know, Chief, you will never change, let us make it an evening to remember."

Chief held up his hands as if in a reverie. "Yes, this room will be transformed, and hopefully Miss Regina, will be happy. I feel a live band will add an excitement to the event, something that a deejay could not really muster."

The daytime manager, smiled," You are right sir, I mean Chief, I can even recommend to you the bands we know and book one for you." And so it was decided that the high life band "Coal city stars international" would perform on the engagement night.

Chief Obi arrives in Enugu and has his first meeting with Regina:

The day after Chief Obi had arrived unceremoniously in Enugu, he paid a visit to the Okafor household in Asata to submit a formal application for marriage to Regina even before he had met her. Although the fiancées had been communicating freely by letter and phone prior to this they had actually never formally met, and as such Chief Obi was obliged to present himself at her fathers compound, so to speak, or his flat rather in Asata for the is purpose of securing the fathers blessings on his suit. The blessing had already been fairly well sealed with the multiple prior transactions between Moses and the Chief which had involved several bank wires and direct money transfers via western union to the benefit of the Okafors'. All these prior transactions made it seem as if nearly it were a house and not a wife that the good chief was purchasing. Nevertheless if the object of the chief's generosity had been to secure the goodwill of the father of his prospective bride, it had literally sealed for him the undying devotion of the whole family.

As the Chiefs' large and ungainly frame swaggered into the room accompanied by his contrasting emaciated cousin even Moses Okafor could not deny that the man was not only ugly and fat but rather pompous. The world can be forgiving of humble men with their physical flaws, but find it hard to disregard the same in the arrogant. Chief Obi was proud of his Doctorate degree in Biology, he was equally proud of the Green card he had, which was merely a by product of his marriage to Alice Rivers the beautiful African American. He did not hesitate to dangle these two facts in front of his future in laws as a carrot and stick before a donkey. This proved to be a successful approach, and before long he had the whole Okafor family including Comfort, and the children laughing and imagining themselves on the streets of New York picking up pieces of silver. The excitement was quite palpable in the inflections of Moses voice, as he got excited his voice became higher pitched nearly sounding like a hyena in the bush in the night. It was amazing how easy it was to hope even in the single room that was called home.

Regina meets the Chief Obi:

The day after the formal introduction in Asata, Chief Obi presented himself as planned at the residence of Mrs. Eugenia Nwafor to meet Regina for the first time. In order to keep the meeting as informal and un-orchestrated as possible, the parents of the girl are to not be involved and only the Aunt is asked to supervise the visit. It was also possible that the parents had wisely decided to absent themselves so as to avoid any possibility of the girl complaining to them on meeting her prospective suitor in person. The Chief presented himself in a white agbada which could barely conceal the significant mounds of flesh that hid underneath. On his right hand side was his emaciated cousin Emeka who seemed to have little else to do other than to accompany his older cousin wherever he might please and acted like a paid companion which he indeed was as he was being well compensated for his time. This compensation was of great value to him as he was a university graduate with neither a job nor a business of any sort. He played the role of a sycophant to the extreme, always laughing at the Chief's jokes, and agreeing with everything the Chief said as if he had no mind of his own. His duty at the fiancée's house had been clearly delineated for him before hand. He was to help to defuse the initial meeting with the fiancée and when the introductions had been formally done at a suitable time he was to excuse himself, so as to leave the two love birds alone.

True enough, as soon as he walked in a morbid silence filled the room, and the girl who was twenty years his junior assiduously avoided his gaze. In utter disbelief she watched the man walk in and her immediate reaction was of disgust. In spite of all her attempts to the contrary she found him repulsive.(and when he takes her hand in his she involuntarily shudders, and the old man in his conceit imagines that she is shivering with delight.) She keeps her eyes fixed on the ground throughout the meeting wondering and rightfully so, why she was never given a photograph of this man before he appeared for then she could have spared him of the long trip.

Mrs. Eugenia who stood up from her chair which was beside Regina's greeted him first; she held out her hand and shook his with a smile on her lips.

"Good Afternoon Ma," He quickly said before she could say anything. "Good afternoon, I take it you must be Mrs. Comfort's older sister Mrs. Eugenia."

"Good afternoon, yes I am".

"This is my cousin Emeka."

"Good afternoon, Ma."

"Good afternoon. This is Regina sitting here, Regina come and greet the Chief as it is you he has come to meet."

Regina rose up slowly from her seat and stretched out her hand to shake the Chief's hand. Instead she found herself pulled with a powerful grip into a firm embrace whilst he cried out "Regina! At last we get to meet."

Her aunt could sense that this embrace was more than the young girl had bargained for and she and pulled the two apart, and for want of anything better to say she said:" Excuse me Chief, you are not married yet, let the girl see you first."

Emeka was slightly embarrassed and cleared his throat, "Yes Chief, this is your first meeting calm down."

Unwillingly the Chief let the girl go and she sat down on a chair as far away as she could from his. She sat with her back straight up obviously totally unable to relax in the company of this stranger who was her fiancée. She recognized the voice, but nothing in the voice that she had heard over the past year matched the body that now stood before her. Truly she had known that he was much older than her, and in all fairness one must admit that she had anticipated him to be advanced in age. However, even she had not imagined that he would be quite that Large and aged beyond his years by his western life style.

"How are you my dear?" were his first words to her when they had been left alone by the cousin and Mrs. Eugenia who had retired to the balcony.

He placed his sweaty palm on her hand and squeezed her hand gently while he spoke.

"I went to the Hotel de Paris yesterday and arranged for the engagement party, I hope the venue meets with your approval."

She let a smile pass her lips,

"The Hotel de Paris is the best Hotel in Enugu. Of course, that would be fine."

"I said, for my little bride only the best would do; and would you believe the Hotel Manager has engaged the Coal City Highlife Band to play live at the occasion. Can you believe Emeka was saying what a waste of money! You know what I said, was Emeka, how often do you get married? I remember distinctly telling him that I wished to make this a night to remember, a night for you and for me."

She smiled again and quietly replied.

"Thank you, Chief; you are so kind and so generous."

"Now tell me," he said not wanting to delay the matter any further, "How do you find me now that you meet me. I mean, I know it is one thing to fall in love with a picture or a voice, but how do you find me now that you see me?"

She pretended to not understand the question.

"I am sorry, I don't quite understand what you mean, we are engaged to be married, and that issue is settled I believe."

"Settled with your father but is it settled with you as well?"

"It is settled with me, Chief, I have always obeyed my father."

"Yes, I understand that obedience." Then he took her hand gently into his, "Can this obedience grow into love do you think?"

"I am sure that is possible chief" and she took back her hand.

At the end of the meeting he left with his cousin slightly disturbed by the meeting. The girl spoke little if at all in his presence yet he had deduced that she was not a shy girl. This left him with the disturbing feeling that the girl was being pressurized into the marriage. He broached the matter with his younger cousin Emeka as they drove away.

"Nna, did you notice this girl she no talk around me at all, he be like say she no fit talk I no know wetin he be."

Emeka who was driving the car that they had borrowed for the chief to use during his stay, shrugged his shoulders.

"Chief you too de worry; he no be him Papa wey don tell you she go marry you, so which one you de?"

"Now days the girls are lucky to find husbands at all as there are no men wey get job, he go good."

"Even I myself, I am not eligible to marry, even though I have my university degree; no job, no house, no car, which lady go follow me? Ah beg, it is all these oyibo people wey go ask wetin be de feelings, feelings? Na feelings wey I go chop? Let me tell you in this town most men are twenty years older than their wives, and they are all in love, the husbands with the wives and the wives with the husbands."

Chief Obi listened. He had been gone so long from home that he had forgotten how things used to be, he had forgotten that it was commonplace for an older man to take a younger wife and to think nothing of it. What the younger women thought nobody knew for sure, but they were all obedient wives who kept their thoughts to themselves.

The engagement night:

The halls of the party room at the Hotel de Paris in Enugu had been decorated with white ribbons that had been attached to the ceilings, forming large boughs sweeping down and then back up in meandering patterns to decorate the ceilings. The tables were covered in white bed sheets which served as linens for the tables and a little pink vase sat atop each table containing a bouquet of pink bougainvilleas. The fans were on full blast in addition to the air conditioner that the room was nearly too cold. The buffet table was overflowing with with jeolloff rice and plantains and roasted goat meat. The band was strumming on their instruments and tuning their guitars and checking the audio equipment to be ready for the event.

"Eh eh Chief Obi oh, Chief Obi oh, eh eh Chief Obi oh Chief Obi Oh'
The lead singer crooned into the microphone the praises of the chief at his engagement party. The Chief would then dutifully get up from his seat and spray the fore head of the lead singer with a one hundred naira bill, and sweating profusely he would return to his seat all the while wiping his brow with a handkerchief.
Overall the evening had turned out to be a rollicking success. The food had been catered, and the bride's family who did not own a motor vehicle of their own had been transported by a taxi chartered for the day; the whole family had arrived, from the smallest to the oldest, all dressed in their Sunday finest. The young children had been beside themselves with excitement, getting one Fanta after the other, and eating until they could stomach no more rice, chicken, and plantain. Mrs. Eugenia Nwafor had arrived with the fiancée and Mrs. Chijioke in tow. In the excitement of the evening, Regina had forgotten the unseemliness of her fiancé; in the dulled lighting of the private party room, Chief Obi could nearly be seen as handsome. Although he never said much to her, his conversations could nearly be interesting. Oh, if only they could stay still in time, and keep this

moment of happiness forever, would they not have seized upon it, them both? Only too soon would the morning come, where the stark realities could not be avoided; the truth that Chief Obi was old enough to be her father, and that in no way was she charmed by him. Yet she had gone through with the engagement, as it seemed as if it were too late to back out.

For Chief Obi there were no doubts whatsoever. He looked at the slim young bride to be, and marveled at the smallness of her waist. Even more marvelous was the thought, that he would soon be married to someone he found so desirable. As the evening wore on, he could not take his eyes off this bride to be. Would that he could have married her sooner...

Comfort wore a nice blue lace up and down which matched the Danshiki of her husband. She had tied a pretty red head tie on her head. The children were wearing matching Ankara outfits which she had had sewn for the preceding Christmas and still fit; it was the same outfit they dutifully brought out every Sunday to go to mass at Holy Ghost Cathedral
. There was a little shakiness in her hand as she drank from the glass of Maltex she had before her. She glanced around the room in sheer disbelief. Many years had passed since she had attended a function in any capacity other than as a cook, and here she was with her small children seated at a table eating jeolloff rice and moi moi. Moses her husband was dancing by himself, in the middle of the dance floor; twirling round in circles with his Danshiki ballooning up around his thighs as it caught the breeze of the fans that blew overhead. From the time Moses had entered the party he had no longer been the sensible Moses, but now he was the Moses with too many drinks in his head. So great had his joy been at the occasion that he had drunk several beers in quick succession.

Regina had gone around the room beside her fiancé greeting all the guests. She wore a sky blue up and down which, though of a different material, matched her mother's and father's out fit nicely. She had danced twice with the Chief much to the excitement of the crowd. The music was too loud to allow for intelligent conversation and at ten o'clock, as previously decided with Mrs. Chijioke and Mrs. Eugenia, the decision was made that they must leave the party before it became too dangerous to be on the road.

Mrs. Eugenia sat down beside, Comfort,
"Congratulations!" And she hugged her sister. For Comfort the whole occasion proved more than she could bear, and she dabbed a few tears from her eyes,
" Sister, I have never seen my Moses so happy so, maybe once at our own wedding, today he looks like a king and feels like one.." she giggled." She continued "Sister, we came in our own car, can you imagine the Chief chartered a taxi for us, it picked us up in Asata at noon and took us to the hotel for the night; as Chief said we could not go back to Asata so late tonight, that it was better we stay the night here tonight, with aircon". Mrs. Eugenia smiled. "I can see the children are quite excited and rightly so, well I and Mrs. Chijioke must soon be leaving and we will be taking Regina with us back home, but that is no reason for the party to stop."
"We will go to bed soon ourselves as the children will need to go to bed".
It was decided that the fiancée and fiancé would meet again in the morning. Chief Obi escorted the company to the car where Mrs. Chijioke's driver was sitting behind the wheel with the engine running. He bowed graciously and turned back inside.

Regina Breaks off her engagement to Chief Obi:

The wonderful Chief had returned to the U.S after completing his engagement. Reassurances had been made to the Okafor's that he would not delay the wedding but had hopes of completing the wedding within the year. In the mean time things returned to near normal in the household of the divorcee Mrs. Eugenia Nwafor. That does not mean that the sadness that haunted her soul had seized, but rather that she had learnt to co exist with her condition in the same way a cancer patient learns to live with the disease without succumbing to hopelessness. Regina had provided a welcome distraction and Mrs. Eugenia enjoyed her company immensely. One morning she had been awakened from her bedroom by cries emanating from the room of Regina.

"Somebody please help me" Regina sobbed,
 "I can't, auntie, I can't love this man, I have tried in every way I can, now please tell me what to do. They all promised me marry him, and you will fall in love with him, but I cannot marry for money. And my father is so upset with me that he has told me not to come home unless I come with Chief Obi. I feel like I am a goat for sale to the highest bidder. When I see him I am filled with a sense of revulsion. I have tried to look past his appearance; I have tried to imagine him in his youth... But nothing works, all I see is the monstrosity he has become. But then that is not all, to make matters worse his behavior parallels that of a buffoon, albeit a pleasant one. Maybe the problem is that I keep comparing him with Michael. An unfair comparison by all means, no one or very few could compare favorably with him. Here, a man whose sensitivity is so heightened that it took our being friends for over a year before he even dared to touch to my hand. Forgive me auntie; maybe if my heart had not been taken already I could have tried. Then I remember the poverty of my parents, and my brothers and sisters, and I feel nearly as if I am obliged to say yes without regard to my own feelings…"
"Nonsense," Mrs. Eugenia said. "Was it not love that attracted your parents to each other in the first place? And in the final analysis there is no amount of wealth that can keep a marriage alive; no it is only love that we have left in the end. I cannot object to you refusing to proceed with the engagement, you must follow your conscience. However, I say this with the caveat that you must not be accepting his gifts any longer either for yourself or your parents, as I feel this would only encourage him to think that perhaps you will change your mind."
Regina looked much relieved and got up from her bed for the first time that morning. It was decided that at the nearest possible opportunity Chief Obi would be informed that the engagement could no longer go forward. As he was in the habit of calling her on Saturday evenings it was decided to await his phone call at which

time Mrs. Eugenia would inform him that her niece could not continue with the marriage.

At four p.m. like clock work Regina's mobile phone rung and she immediately handed the phone over to Mrs. Eugenia.

"Hello. Hello." Mrs. Eugenia said.

Chief Obi was in good spirits. "Good evening Auntie Eugenia, how are you?"

"I am fine and I hope you are fine."

"Yes, I have been getting the house ready for my new bride; I am looking forward to our being together."

"I see." said Mrs. Eugenia not knowing how to break the news gently.

"Yes he continued" "I am so looking forward to having a woman in the house again and a real one this time."

"Does that mean that your first wife was not real?"

"Oh no, she was as real as real can be ma, believe me, maybe too real for me. There is no harm in having a bit of an imagination."

"I guess not". She continued still not being able to say anything.

Regina was motioning frantically in the background pointing to the ground. She pointed with her index finger of the right hand towards the ground.

"Ta Ta bu tata. Today na today."

And then she waved her hands frantically back and forth to signal no, when being motioned to come and take the phone. She finally had no choice but to accept the phone, and hurriedly while she still had the courage she blurted out:

" I am so sorry Chief Obi, I can no longer marry you, please accept my apologies; I thought we could make a go of it, but I am now decided that I must marry in the church and that I cannot marry a divorcee, does that make sense to you.?'

He thought it did make sense, though he stated he was not averse to marrying in church either.

"You don't understand, Chief, the Catholic Church will not allow me to marry a divorcee in the church." The matter was settled.

The Chief felt no need to pander pleasantries any longer. He felt ill used, the bride to be's parents had already benefited considerably from his generosity, and he was too proud to request for a return of the gifts; most of which had been in cash, and there was certainly no cash to give back. Over the course of the evening he came to grips with the rejection. He who had so recently fancied that he was remarried, with a young and attractive bride, the envy of all his friends. He had already imagined the sweet aroma of freshly made egusi soup wafting out of the kitchen of his house, and a table set with food ready to be eaten on coming home at the end of a hard days work. He had imagined the love of a devoted and obedient wife from home… now none of that was to be. Or if it was to be, it most certainly was not to be Regina

Barely twenty four hours after the Chief had received the dreadful news of the breaking of the engagement by Regina he felt recovered enough to lick his wounds and to call Mr. Moses on the phone to complain about the behavior of his daughter and to ask for a return of the gifts that he had sent thinking that they were his in laws to be. To make matters even worse, neither Regina, nor her Aunt Mrs. Eugenia, had seen it fit nor necessary to alert Mr. Moses about the change in circumstance. And as such, Mr. Moses was taken completely by surprise when an angry Chief confronted him on the phone. It took a whole five minutes of interchanges before Mr. Moses could ascertain that Regina had broken off the engagement without her father's permission. He now found him self arguing with the Chief about the 200,000 Naira he had been sent the week prior; and the Chief wanted the money back immediately, but Moses had already spent the money. This being more money than Moses could make in a month there was little chance of him ever being able to pay the money back, despite his good intentions.
When he got off the phone with the Chief he was livid, and he called his wife into the courtyard, where he proceeded to give her a complete dressing down about the unsuitableness of the companionship of their oldest daughter with, the divorcee and fallen woman, Mrs. Eugenia, who was now accused of masterminding the plot of Regina's dissension.
"You see, Comfort, I told you, can it be good for Regina to be staying with a divorcee? Now she wants to destroy the marriage of even the unmarried? I think she must be a enemy of marriage;

herself having this bad experience she now thinks that all marriages are bad."

Comfort was not very comfortable with her husband's line of thought, although she was not sure what to believe.

Then Mr. Moses Okafor made his declaration of war, he drew the line in the sand and dared anyone to cross it.

"I will call Regina, this is not acceptable, she must marry this man and the engagement must go forward. This man is calling me for a return of the 200,000 naira. Where on earth am I going to get that kind of money to repay him?"

Comfort agreed with her husband. And it was decided that in the morning Comfort would go to her sister's house before she went to her stall at the market so that she could give Regina a message from her father.

Regina writes a letter to Chief Obi under duress.

The outcome of Comfort's visit with Regina was that a letter was sent to the Chief . It went like this:

Dearest Chief,

How are you? I hope you are fine. I have thought of everything and have come to the conclusion that I have made a dreadful mistake by breaking up our engagement. In fact my father has made his displeasure of the current situation known to me and has asked me to formally retract what I had said earlier about breaking off our engagement. I have called your cell phone and your home phone many times but the message is that your phone line has been disconnected. Could you please call my cell phone at the nearest possible time as my number is unchanged so that we can discuss this matter further,

Your loving fiancée,

Regina.

Moses wrote a letter as well on a separate piece of paper.

Dear Chief,
Please read the letter enclosed from Regina who has changed her mind and wants to proceed with the wedding. We have been trying to contact you to no avail. Please call my cell as we are anxious to settle the wedding date,
Sincerely,
Mr. Moses Okafor, your future father in law.

The two letters were sent by mail to the Chief's home address in the U.S.A., and the family waited patiently for a response from the Chief. It took three weeks for the Chief to receive the letter, and within moments of reading the letter he was back on the phone talking this time first to Moses, who he needed to reassure him verbally that the coast was clear, before he made any attempts to call Regina. In the meantime, Regina was instructed that under no circumstances was she to make any rash decision before consulting with her parents, in regards to the Chief. Oddly enough, even though Mrs. Eugenia had been accused of influencing her decision no attempt had been made to repatriate her form her aunts home, as they felt that subjecting their eldest daughter to the cramped conditions at home would make her less likely to listen to the father's authority.

The Girl is 'already taken':

Michael Asimnobi was knocking on the door to the flat on Chime Avenue. He seemed to be perturbed, as he knocked quicker than usual. Two days prior, his suit had been out rightly rejected by Mr. Moses Okafor. He had been told that Regina was, unfortunately, already engaged. In vain were the reassurances given to the girls father, wherein was stated, that he in fact was there at Regina's request; the father appeared to not hear, and went on to say that he Michael, was not a suitable candidate, and moreover, that the girl was "taken already." Mr. Moses Okafor had insisted outrightly that the girl was committed to the "Chief", and that the matter was settled. All attempts by Michael to persuade the father otherwise were in vain. He had finally given up and had left.

Many discussions later it had been decided between the two lovers that they would continue to meet, albeit on an unofficial basis. And it was during these visits that she poured out her heart to him and he poured out his heart to her. He chose to no longer visit her in the evenings, but instead, to come when Mrs. Eugenia was out; and they would sit in the love seat in the little living room.   In all fairness, Mrs. Eugenia had no idea that this was going on under her roof. She was aware of the commotion that had occurred when the engagement to the Chief had initially been broken; but then her niece had, after the reinstatement of her broken engagement, retreated into her shell; and from then on she had only said nice things about the Chief, and nothing at all about the young lover. As such, Mrs. Eugenia had assumed that the girl's obedience to her father had got the better of her, and that she was now intent upon doing the best for her family.

On this day he was seated by himself on a chair by the café style dining table, and his voice was becoming more urgent in its tone, and there was weariness in his brow, which clearly betrayed the stress he was feeling.

"I have arranged all the details down to the last", he said totally unable to contain his excitement, "and I think I have it planned; we will have to leave the day before the wedding with a coach for Benin. I have my cousin who lives in Benin and I know they will never be able to trace us in such a large city."

"The wedding will have to be arranged after we have settled there, and there is nothing to worry about."

"What of work, and money and the like? How on earth are we to support ourselves?" she interjected.

" I have not thought so far, but my father will set us up to open a business of sorts, this is the promise he has made me, all along; a business, even if small should be a way out ."

Michael Asimnobi was a person of great self confidence. He cherished no doubts about his intellectual capacity. On the other hand he was totally naive about the effect of his physique, and manners upon the opposite sex. Unlike most dashing young men with a reasonable amount of savoir faire and worldliness, he had no predilection towards profligacy. All these virtues and natural attributes of his, had turned him into an insurmountable foe for the Chief. He knew that he was intelligent, however, he was modest about his physical appearance, seemingly ignorant of the profound effect he had upon the opposite sex. He was over six feet tall, and he had long well proportioned limbs, which had the right amount of musculature to make him attractive. Although his biceps was well defined, his triceps was not over large, and his chest was broad but not to the point that he was intimidating. This was combined with a manner and a composure which was gentle. He radiated a softness. From his childhood he had been brought up in his father's village, being the last born of a family of seven, he had been surrounded by unconditional love from his infancy. At an early age he had been sent away to attend the Loyola Jesuit College outside Abuja, as his father had worried that the quality of the education in the village would be below the standard required for admission to university. education.

Michael and Regina take a walk in Okpara square:

There is a place in Enugu inside independence layout, opposite the gate to the governor's mansion called Okpara square. And it was to this park that on a nice Saturday morning in September, when the air was still cool, and dew drops were forming on the leaves of the grass that Michael took Regina. The Bougainvilleas in bright red, and orange and pink were flowering from their bushes, and the air was filled with the soft fragrance of blooming white Gardenias which intoxicated the air with their bewitching fragrance. Up above the flame of the forest tree was also in bloom and the bright red flowers were surrounded by the fan like leaves . The air was still and

Okpara square was as busy as usual on a weekend morning. Here and there could be seen a few people trying to get their morning walk in. For the most part the park was empty. The privileged few who needed the exercise the most had long since abandoned coming to the park for exercise, out of fear of being an easy prey for kidnappers. In direct contradistinction, the poor who could move freely around without precautions, had no such need of any extra movement, and for the most part lacked the time to be spent on the pleasantries of life; their time being consumed in a day to day existence which could only have been described as precarious at best.

The handsome Michael wore a light blue dress shirt, and a pair of slacks of tan color, and the object of his affections wore a Ankara blouse and matching wrapper skirt which was orange and pink and had large flowering designs which complemented the surroundings. The young man had his arm curled through her arm and they walked in seeming perfect harmony......

Michael had become increasingly uncomfortable with his visits to Regina at the home of her aunt Mrs. Eugenia. It was not that he felt unwelcome per se, but he had felt a general distaste to going there ever since his surprise encounter with the Chief at her residence. The existence of Chief Obi had been a complete surprise to the young man. Mrs. Eugenia had brushed this off with the peremptory assertion that

"Any young man should not assume that his suit should be without healthy competition; and that indeed, one can assume that a desirable female will not want for a multitude of vying suitors."

It was more the idea that her father had promoted the suit of the Chief, and that in effect Regina was now formally engaged to the Chief, a fact that the Chief had made clear, even if Regina had not, at their meeting.

The meeting had been a tumultuous one. Michael had arrived at Mrs. Eugenia Nwafor's residence the day after the engagement party, to meet Regina and the Chief alone in the sitting room with Mrs. Eugenia and Emmanuel waiting on the balcony. On his arrival he had found the two seated beside each other with the chief's hand on Regina's shoulder. Regina had been dressed in a white dress,

and had quickly become flustered upon his arrival and had sprung to her feet,
" Michael, I did not know you were coming!" She had greeted him.
The chief had looked at the young man, and then looked at her, searching in her face for some clue as to the identity of the young man.
"I'm sorry" he had said simply. "I assumed you would know I was coming as I did not hear from you the last few days."
The chief, who had been largely ignored by the young man, was just as confused about the unexpected interruption of his rendez vous, stood up and extended his hand with a friendly patronizing smile.
"May I introduce myself to you, I am Chief Dr. Obi; I hold a Phd from the University of Illinois."
Michael smiled back "Good morning, I am Michael Asimnobi."

Mrs. Eugenia had looked in from the window of the balcony that looked into the living room, and having noticed that Michael had arrived she had quickly entered the room.
"Ah Michael you are welcome, come and join us on the balcony; what can we get you to drink?"
She had ushered Michael to the balcony, as this was the day before the Chief was to travel back to the U.S and she wanted to give the fiancé a chance to spend time with her fiancé. Then unexpectedly the girl had announced :
" It is okay auntie, why don't we all come out on the balcony and have some fresh air/"
The engaged couple had followed the group onto the balcony and there they had stood by the railing looking down on Chime Avenue and had observed the traffic. The Chief had been disappointed at the interruption of their tete a tete, but nevertheless he had insisted on standing beside Regina on the balcony.
It had been on the balcony that the Chief had talked about the engagement party. The young Michael had barely been able to hide his shock at this announcement

………They walked together side by side on one of the walkways heading towards the government house. He had her hand in his, and he was trembling as they walked.

"Why did you not warn me ahead of time of the Chief and the engagement party?"

He asked her in earnest.

"Please forgive me; this whole engagement thing was not my idea. It was a year ago that my father approached me that there was a man who they wanted me to correspond with who lived abroad. I had no choice but to agree. The next thing was that they said he was coming to Enugu and wanted to marry me."

"Well could you not have said no?"

"I did say no." she reassured him. "But you do not know my father; he does not accept that I do not want an arranged marriage. He says that this is not really an arranged marriage, but merely a set of introductions."

"Introductions my foot"

"He keeps insisting that I am free to refuse, but then in reality, I have no freedom at all; the freedom is merely theoretical."

"Regina, I love you, I have always wanted to marry you, now my hand has been forced, and I can wait no longer, for if I wait I will loose you."

"Will you give me permission to go to your father to seek his permission?"

"Yes, maybe if you go your self he will see that you are a better match than the Chief, maybe if we go together then his heart will melt?"

"Tell me," he continued "Tell me that you love me too; reassure me, that all I have experienced, has not been merely one sided; reassure me that your heart is mine, no matter what engagements they have arranged for you." Then he took her in his arms and whispered into her ear in between kissing her on her cheek, "Run away with me! Just promise me that we will be together no matter what, and then I can stand by and make arrangements that we will escape together."

The road to Lagos.:

The summer vacation had come and gone without any trip to Lagos materializing, mainly as she had been unable to afford the tickets on her salary. Finally when the Christmas vacation had arrived, Margaret had tired of hearing the excuses for her not coming to Lagos and had persuaded Charlie to send five bus tickets for the family to spend Christmas with them in Lagos. The tickets had been eagerly received. In the old days Mr. Charlie Obiora would have taken his family back to Abagana for the Christmas Holidays, however, with the recent spate of kidnappings in Anambra state the family had abandoned the village visits until further notice. It would have been different, perhaps if his mother and father were still alive; but as they had long since abandoned this earth, the family home stood locked up all year waiting for Charlie or his brothers to come for the holidays. It was so the compound would have to be kept locked up until the government or the vigilantes or the people them selves could decide that the kidnappings had to stop.

No one really knew nor understood the genesis of this malaise which was to eat at the very core of the heart of the society. There was speculation about whether this was a class war, or whether this was a form of revolt of the people against a government which had some how forgotten the plight of the ordinary man.

" Christmas in Lagos," Chinedu had said to Afam, " Ahh Christmas away from here what a relief."

He was relieved because Henrietta had just in the week before Christmas given birth to a bouncing baby Boy and had named him Christian Junior. This was a name that should have been given to his first son, and the slight did not go un noticed by his first family. Mr. Christian had also informed his first family, that Henrietta was too busy to entertain over the Christmas holidays and suggested that they might be happier at the flat on Chime Avenue. That had been the last the children had heard from the father, and as such the tickets from Uncle Charlie were well received.

In reality there was no love lost between the children and Henrietta. For the first few months of their fathers marriage to his mistress there had been an unspoken truce between the children and their step mother. This time had merely served as a time for them all to test the waters and to feel each other out. This truce had by now been long since abandoned, and in it's stead there reared an undeclared act of war which had seemingly been agreed upon by the parties involved. As the children had made their presence so burdensome to the step mother, who had by this time become heavily pregnant, Mr. Christian had found himself in a difficult position. On the one hand he did enjoy his children from his first wife, in as much as a manner as a father can enjoy the society of his children, but on the other hand he had to live at peace with his new wife; and was fearful that his children might actually succeed in driving away the one woman he loved.. As such he had come to the decision that at this point at least the children could spend more time with their mother and that if they needed him he was just a mobile phone call away.

There is a general feeling in the east that once you cross the Niger River Bridge from Asaba to Onitsha that you are home. And the converse is equally true that once you cross the bridge from Onitsha to Asaba you have sureptiously left home, and entered, so to speak, into a no man's land. The argument could always be made that since they still spoke some form of "Igbo" in Asaba, that you were not too far from home; but this was more a theoretical argument, as from Asaba to Agbor, no matter what language was spoken, and regardless of whether an Igbo man thought he could understand it or not, he was always informed that the speakers were NOT Igbo, with an emphasis upon NOT. And furthermore, was reassured that the language was NOT Igbo. And as such, Mrs. Eugenia Nwafor kept her four children close by her as the luxury bus made its winding way through the Midwestern part of the country heading for Lagos. They had made the spectacular crossing across the Niger River at high noon, as the sun shone overhead with the river reflecting bright rays of light upwards. To be certain the River was more than a mile wide at this juncture with sand bars pushing out from the river banks which themselves were covered in profuse vegetation. Oddly enough it was obvious to the naked eye that there was not much of the town on the River bank, but instead the town had set itself up inland from the river bank, perhaps as a safety precaution from flood, or perhaps this had been a matter of necessity in the days of slavery, as a River provided easy access for the marauders who traded up and down the river dealing in human flesh.

This fear of the past history of slavery had pervaded the subconscious and one could never feel completely safe whilst in the village of another, let alone in a town where you did not speak the language. And this fear grew more and more in the mind of Mrs. Eugenia as the bus entered the city of Benin. The bus stopped at a small non descript hotel for the driver to take a break and for the passengers to alight that needed to visit the bathroom. Outside the windows of the bus there was a fervent market activity with buying and selling of boiled, eggs, and water, and bananas and other snacks. A whole little market had come to thrive by this bus stop and the hawkers swarmed each bus on arrival with their trays balanced on their heads. By the time the Bus reached the town of Ore she was totally paranoid, and would not let the children move from their seats until the bus entered the station in Lagos.

The taxi drove the Nwafor's up to the front gate of the block of flats in Ikeja which the Obiora's had rented in Lagos. Mrs. Margaret Obiora, and Ify and Eugenia ran to the gate to meet them as they were making their way into the compound with their bags. There were hugs and kisses exchanged between the sisters and the cousins and they were led into the living room where a large welcome feast awaited them.
The Obiora family flat was located in a newer part of Ikeja, and the flat was located in a complex of six flats. The external of the building was decorated with a faux stone pattern, with the grey stones outlined in white, forming a nice warm façade. The interior floors were made of the terrazzo with pretty marble chips of white and black and red against a nice grey background . the furniture was upholstered in a deep burgundy, which complemented the heavy velvet curtains with an interior lace panel which provided some privacy to the interior living room and also helped to filter out some of the sunlight. On the side tables of the living room stood little coasters and on the main center table were some vases which appeared to be of oriental origin.. On The walls of the entrance way was placed a wedding photo of the husband and wife, and a more recent family photo showing the husband and wife and the five offspring in matching regalia, all smiling before the camera. a table off to a corner which was adjacent to the entry way served as a

memorial to older family members who had passed on, and here there was arranged a set of photos of deceased family members, and the father and mother of Charlie, and likewise of Margaret's parents..

They proceeded immediately to the dining room, and there it had been set in a formal manner; Fine china of white with gold borders was set with newly polished silverware. A bright yellow table cloth set the tone for the celebration.

The menu had been chosen by Mrs. Margaret Obiora to please the tired travels, and as such she offered at table a wider variety than usual. There was rice and stew with fries plantains for the children; and then she had a yam pottage for the adults who might prefer it. As it was a holiday season she brought out a fruit cake for desert and had a fruit salad of oranges and bananas and pine apple which her cook had decorated with sweetened shredded coconut.

 Charlie was as usual away on business, and the two sisters sat beside each other talking all the while totally oblivious to their children who were exchanging stories of their own about school and the like.

    Only too soon had night fallen and the younger girls were falling asleep in front of a video when their mothers gathered them together and proceeded to guide the sleepy heads to bed.

"I am awake Mother," Henrietta had reassured her mother opening her eyes wide and rubbing them with her hands at the same time. Mrs. Margaret laughed.

"Was it not just now that I woke you up from the sofa? All of you have fallen asleep, and without having a bath."

"Auntie please can we not watch a little longer,"

"Certainly not," their mother had replied, "tomorrow is another day and we will have a lot of time to watch the videos."

Christmas in Lagos:

In many ways it had felt strange to Mrs. Eugenia to spend Christmas in Lagos, the town that never slept. But then she had had to come to terms with so many different things since her marriage had failed. She had done well for herself overall, yet the obstacles she had encountered had been considerable, and in reality nothing had been easy. It had been difficult to muster up the courage to leave her former husband, but then after she had left, she had discovered that the act of leaving was probably the easiest thing of all. It was what had followed that had proved so difficult. Nevertheless, with the arrival of Christian's new son from Henrietta, her old wounds had been opened once again.. It brought back memories of her own children when they had been born, and the total lack of assistance she had received from Christian, who had now apparently become very different. In any case, there was nothing to be done; she hoped the change of pace, and place would help her to regain her composure; she hoped that somewhere or somehow she would once again be able to find some meaning in her life.

As she watched the dynamics of the Obiora house hold it became starkly visible how different the atmosphere here was from how her marital home had been. All the criticisms Mrs. Margaret had made over the years about her family now seemed to make sense. The whole house was suffused in a warmth that in many ways could only have been instituted by Divine providence. The love that existed between Mrs. Margaret and Charlie after all the years of marriage could only have been described as beautiful. It pervaded every interaction of the spouses and by default affected every member of the household in a positive manner. Whereas the Nwafor children could often be heard quarreling in loud and obnoxious tones, the Obiora's spoke softly to one another, and one would have thought that the three youngest daughters were singing a song had one listened to their exchanges, so beautiful were their voices and calculated their tones.

The return of Charlie from Cotonou the day before Christmas caused the whole house to be filled with anticipation, confirming the quick approaching festivities. Mrs. Margaret Obiora had used more care than usual with her toilette on the morning of her husbands return. She had drenched herself in his favorite perfume Chanel Number 5, and had put on one of her nicer george wrappers with a matching blouse in her favorite gold color. On this day her lips had been accentuated in a deep red. She contrasted sharply with the appearance of Mrs. Eugenia whose make up consisted of a face powder and some poorly placed eye liner, and was wearing her trade mark black skirt, with a white blouse, that was no longer quite white, and the black jacket casually draped over everything, in an effort to convey some semblance of formality about her appearance. Under normal circumstances, she reserved such efforts for work, or for the charity meetings. However, here in the beautifully furnished and ornately decorated flat of her younger sister, she felt the need to dress up to match the environment.

Mr. Charlie Obiora had not met his sister in law in several years. Despite the fact that he often travelled through Enugu frequently on his way to Onitsha for business, he never made an effort to see his sister in law, never having felt any undue attachment to her, or to her former husband, Christian. He had felt slightly inferior to the well educated Christian; however, after he had amassed his fortune, and his business had done well, he no longer felt any need to make an effort to befriend a man who had previously regarded him with disdain and as his unequal. After greeting his wife with a kiss, he proceeded to take in the scene before him; and he could not help but to notice that his sister in law had aged dramatically since he had seen her last. The air of sadness, which had always surrounded her, had been further deepened by her divorce; and her frame had increased considerably in size, with a weight gain that had accompanied her depression. The ill fitting suit only served the more to emphasize her pitiable state.
He smiled at her hiding his true feelings behind his mien,
"Mrs. Eugenia, you have finally made it to Lagos. Maybe now Maggie can rest now that she has seen you here with everybody."
Mrs. Eugenia returned the smile.
"Thank you, broder, for the tickets, and for your hospitality. You can not know how much we all have been looking forward to this trip, and it came not a moment too soon."
"I hope not too late, either," he continued. "Tell me, how is Enugu?"
"Not much different from the rest of the east, I daresay. They say it is better, but I am not quite sure what they are referring to. Are they talking about the supply of power? There is still no light. Or could it

be the price of food? When a loaf of bread can now easily be bought for 200 Naira?"

Charlie laughed at this sordid rendition, and his wife could not resist laughing as well.

"Never mind Mrs. Eugenia," he said, "this is Christmas and we will think of happy places and happy things, and tomorrow we will worry about the power supply and the cost of bread."

"Yes," his wife agreed and stood up and walked over to where her sister sat and placed her hands in her sister hands, " Yes for today is the day before Christmas, and for one day we will put all our sorrows behind us and be determined to be happy."

"If only it were so easy to be happy at will, would not then the whole world be filled with laughter." She replied.

And Charlie laughed again, not sure of what to say he left the sisters to themselves, for he was a man who had no trouble in viewing the positive side of things, an eternal optimist and he was wont if he'd let the sorrows of Mrs. Eugenia, or anyone for that matter put a damper on his spirits.

Christmas in Lagos:

For an Igbo man who resides in Lagos, there could be few things more annoying than having to spend Christmas in Lagos. That is not to say that he does not enjoy living in the center of the action and whatever that may entail. He may have been born and raised in the heart of Ajegunle, or Surulere, nevertheless, he knows that his home is elsewhere. The way Nigeria operates is strictly by tribal affiliation and for the Igbo man that means going to his home town for Christmas. Now Charlie Obiora found himself for the second year in a row spending Christmas in Lagos, the last place he had wanted to be at this time of the year. He had always enjoyed the annual pilgrimage when he would gather his family around and they would proceed with the driver to Abagana in his car, loaded with gifts for his relatives and friends. At Abagana they would stay in the compound that Charlie's father had set up with small bungalows for each of his four sons. Needless to say, it was a festive occasion with sundry parties taking place all over the village, and of course there was the masquerades who went through the town and danced accompanied by the drummers and flute players.

Unfortunately, too many close calls with near disasters had been reported over the preceding two years. Gory tales of kidnappings and assassinations had been for a while every day affairs on the newspapers. As a sensible man he had determined that there was no need to tempt fate at least in this regard, and as such it had become time again to celebrate Christmas in Lagos.

The sights and sounds of Lagos were overwhelming. This metropolis of millions sttod proud and ready to bring the unaware to their knees at a momnet's notice. The streets were teeming with activity and motor vehicles and large over crowded buses all the while being intercepted by motor cycle drivers and street hawkers darting in and out. From the street stalls there were canteens with out door kitchens cooking for the tired travelers, and stroes selling watyer in plastic pouches which had been cooled to a desirable temperature.

Even the gutters were overflowing with refuse of all kinds and covered with a green slimy layer of putrid algae. To the children this was all exciting and they watched the sightjs as they drove thorugh ikorodu road to their aunt's flat which was in a relatively new area in Ikeja.

Chinedu and Afam were the same age as Chas Jr. the first child of Mrs Margaret Obiora. He was two years ahead in school and was in the same year of SS6 as Chinedu and was seeking admission to the University as well. The boys were off by themselves playing table tennis on a table in the back garden which was under a Guava tree which provided shade. In the evenings the boys were mostly playing a variety of video games in Chas Jrs's room, whilst the younger girls seemed to have monopolized the television in the living room, and were watching a seemingly endless series of movies. Until the day after Christmas, when Mr. Charlie Obiora decided that a trip to the beach was the thing to do. The children were overcome with excitement, as it promised to be a spectacular and sunny day at the beach. Overhead there loomed a few ominous clouds, but no one would put off the trip to Bar Beach for the day.

On their arrival at the beach the group found a small locally made hut to rent. It was made from dried palm leaf fronds which were held together by raffia, and this was made to form a roof and walls. By the seaside the open expanse of the Atlantic Ocean was visible as far as the eye could see. At the bar beach the waves were large, and came crashing down on to the sand beneath their feet in white turbulent surf, which lapped at their toes. As none of the group was particularly strong at swimming it was decided to only roll up their trousers and to wade in the surf. The young girls were walking down the beach with the maid and Charlie to supervise them; whilst the boys were deemed old enough to take care of themselves and were allowed more freedom to wander away on their own, but only after the admonishment of not going into the ocean above their knees.

The two sisters were thus left alone and at peace to walk along the beach. Mrs. Eugenia Nwafor felt the sea breeze against her cheeks, and it blew her hair up into an untidy mess. Yet she felt that here, by the water she could stay forever and perhaps the heavens could heal her soul here better than it ever could in the dry hot air of Enugu in the dry season. Out over the sea she saw the sea melt into the sky and the white clouds danced above and the sun glittered down in a scene of unparalleled beauty. It was during moments like this, that she could not but help but reaffirm her belief in God, and His Divine purpose. Although she could not pretend to understand His ways, yet who was she mere mortal as herself, and could only in all humility, accept what little solace He gave her when He pleased. And as she walked arm in arm with her sister she could not help but confide this thought to her dear sister.
"My dearest sister, how happy I am today to be walking here on this beach…and to be surrounded by such beauty and to have you my most favorite person in the world beside me. It is in moments like these, that I thank God for the little things, because, sometimes I am not sure if there will be anything else, or anything more. To me the redemption is in the colors of the sun and the water, to once again be bale to see beyond the pain has overcome my soul."

"When we were young and Papa and Mama would always tell us that one day we would have our day to shine and we would be married. In fact, now that I think of everything, I think the whole society programmed us in this belief. Look how it affected us all! Comfort ran away at the age of sixteen and married before all of us! It was all backwards, I the first daughter, was married the last, and the last was married the first."

Margaret laughed.

"Yes, and much good it has done for Comfort, who has no education herself."

"I have often thought of that, and I am not certain that my own education has been of much use, yes I have a job, for now at least, but for how much longer? The reality is that at any moment in time I can be recalled, and replaced. At least Comfort owns her own stall and has more job security than I.'

That is all well, and good, and now tell me, about the preparations for the wedding between Regina and the Chief; tell me about her dress, and the plans for the party. How I wish I could have attended, but Charlie has refused to allow me to go to the east again just now, I think he does not approve of the marriage as e has said that he knows the Chief is a divorcee and he does not really feel this is appropriate for Regina. And I know it will be a court wedding only.

Well, she will wear a white dress even though it will be a court wedding. However, the reception will be much smaller than the engagement party as the Chief has said that he will return later to do the real thing.

The wind caressed her cheeks, and the cool air held her in its gentle embrace, and she could feel the sorrow draining out of her soul. In its stead there was a lightness of spirit and she seized upon the moment greedily to extract with an unrequited urgency every morsel of joy that could be gleaned from it. On an impulse she ran up to the boy Chinedu, and held him in one arm, and Afam in the other, and walked down the beach with them arm in arm.

The boys had found some ponies with their owners and paid to take a ride down the beach taking turns on the rides. The girls returned with their father and had hands full of sea shells which they were putting up against their ears and listening to the sound of the sea.

Then they went to a shed and bought fresh coconuts cut from the tree and opened in front of them with coconut milk and they bought suya.

A send off party for Mrs. Eugenia and family:

It so happened, that the day before the families departure to Enugu, Charlie decided that he would have a small get together for his in laws ,; a send off , so to speak. Mrs. Margaret Obiora quite liked the idea. It was a nice way to round off the holiday with a few friends, and some dancing and some music. A family oriented party was planned, and there were three families invited. The Okekes, and the Obi's and the Okoro's had been invited, all of the families had children of about the same age and it promised to be a hilarious time. Of note was that Mr. Oke Ejiofor, the lonesome widower, whose wife of thirty years, had died three years prior, and whom, Charlie thought, would be a decent man to introduce to his sister in law, was also invited. Mr.Oke Ejiofor was no spring chicken, but then neither was Mrs. Eugenia, he thought to himself; and he glossed over the fact that though Mrs. Eugenia was old, she was barely 44 years of age, and he was introducing her to a man, who was over sixty years of age, yet, he was deemed an 'equitable match' Mr. Oke Ejiofor was not bad looking considering his age However, his hair betrayed tinges of grey all over, and the beard that he sported was mostly grey itself, making one think he was older than his age. Moreover, he dated himself by wearing clothes which were out of style, and his face was decorated by a pair of brown rimmed spectacles which were large and the lenses were thick magnifying his eyes when looked upon. He was a quiet man who said little. Having retired from the civil service, he was a dignified man nevertheless and he sported a sports like jacket of hounds tooth pattern, that was quite becoming. His loneliness was amplified by the fact that even though he had two children, they were both abroad, and as such he really had no close relatives nearby except the Obiora's. Charlie was related to him by being a nephew of his. The widower sat quietly in a corner and watched the proceedings with interest; without becoming directly involved. Charlie was the Dee jay for the occasion, and also seemingly, the life of the party; and he danced on several occasions with his wife, and also with the wives of the other guests whose husbands seemed more intent on drinking than on socializing.

The sights in the room were to die for, with all colors and shades of the rainbow being amply displayed on the dresses of the females guests, who were all dressed up in their Christmas finery. Not to be outdone, Mrs. Margaret Obiora was looking dashing in a bright red George wrapper with a contrasting blouse in a brown lace; Mrs. Eugenia Nwafor presented herself in a new black dress, not having the courage to wear any lighter color, lest it show the size of her frame to a disadvantage. Mr Oke Ejiofor finally summoned the courage and asked Mrs. Eugenia if she would dance a slow dance with him. She agreed, and above the music he introduced himself to her again, and asked her how her trip to Lagos had been. And he lamented about the insecurities in the east, which had made the party possible in the first place, as none of the party goers had been able to return home for the Christmas.

Due to the sobriety of her dress, and her general sparing use of makeup, for some reason, he had forgotten that she was actually a divorcée, thinking that she was a widow like himself, and as such he had poised to her the improbable question, " Now tell me how long have you been widowed for?" Mrs. Eugenia Nwafor had been taken aback by this faux pas and had quickly corrected him. "I am not widowed, sir, no I am a divorcee". Mr. Oke Jideofor had cleared his throat in embarrassment, "Pardon me, I don't know why I thought you were a widow." He lied, knowing full well that he had thought so as she was dressed in black from head to toe. "Forgive me, Ma'am," he had continued, "But am I mistaken in saying, that these colors are reserved for the mourning and the professionals who are either called to the law professions, or bankers? Now might I guess that you may belong to one of these professions?"

She had proceeded to correct him, that she was neither a banker nor a lawyer, and his apologies had been profuse. He had insisted that to be forgiven for his lack of chivalry that she must allow him to take her to lunch when he came to Enugu next.

t promise to go out with him to lunch at a future date whenever he came to Enugu.

Mrs. Eugenia returns to Enugu after spending Christmas in Lagos:

The harmattan came late that year, and by the time the family was to return to Enugu, a swarm of dust had descended on the southern part of the country making the air heavy with dust; the sun was barely visible as a round shiny disc far in the distance. The Lagos airport was forced to close and the flights had to be diverted, and the offices of the luxury coaches serving Eastern Nigeria were overflowing with passengers. The family was lucky to still get a seat and started the long ride home to Enugu.

A wedding fit for a Chief:

It was a Thursday morning and Mrs. Eugenia Nwafor was off, she woke up early in the morning and after having her usual bucket bath she sat down to enjoy her customary breakfast. On holiday mornings she liked to take her time and get up a little later than her normal weekday routine. The maid Miriam who slept on a mat in the kitchen was still asleep when she went into the kitchen to get some bread and tea. She stepped gently around the sleeping maid in an effort to not awaken her, and put some water on to boil at the kerosene stove. The loaf was retrieved from a container. All the while Miriam did not stir. She set everything on a tray and carried it into the dining table. After completing her breakfast, On arising from her seat, she noticed that the large gate which was placed across the entrance door at night was open. Strange, she had thought ,as it was the duty of Miriam to open the gate but the gate was already open and Miriam was still asleep. Puzzled she walked across the room to the front door and after ascertaining that it was indeed locked she went in to check on Regina who slept in the other bedroom. On entering the room it became immediately obvious that Regina was not in the room and that she had packed all of her belongings. Mrs. Eugenia was overcome by a panic, the girl was supposed to be getting ready for her marriage to the chief which had been scheduled for the following Tuesday. The white wedding gown alone was left in the room hanging from a hanger. A note was left on the des and a gold engagement style ring with a small diamond in the center was beside the note.

.

"Dear auntie," it read, "Thank you for everything. Please forgive me for not being able to say goodbye to you. I am writing this note to let you know that I am safe and that I have left town with Michael. We are to be married at the nearest possible date. Please tell my mother and father not to worry. I cannot marry the Chief. I have left the wedding gown and the engagement ring in the room so that you can return them to him.
Love,
Regina."
Without any further to do Mrs. Eugenia Nwafor quickly dressed up and went down to Chime Avenue to secure a Okada to take her to Asata.
She arrived at the Okafor household only to meet the children alone at home, and both Moses and Comfort had gone out. She asked about whether their mother was at the market stall and was told that she had gone to cook for a wedding taking place on Zik Avenue at one of the popular hotels there. Mr. Moses had gone to the market to buy drinks for the weeding party planned for the next day.

In the back yard of the Hotel, the catering team was busy at work preparing for a wedding party that was to be held there later in the evening Three large pots were being used to cook and were

Comfort was stirring a huge pot over a fire, the contents of which was bubbling and steaming up into her face. She stirred the pot with a giant spoon more akin to a log.

 Comfort was standing above the large cast black cast iron pot in which a large red stew was steaming up into the air. She was singing a song and stirring her pot with wanton abandon, on the other side of the compound there were two other pots with their contents being watched over by her cooking mates. She looked up from her pot and saw what seemed to be her older sister Mrs. Eugenia who was walking hurriedly towards her.

Comfort was standing above the large black cast iron pot in which bubbled a large red stew which was steaming up into the air. She was singing a song and stirring her pot with wanton abandon, on the other side of the compound there were two other pots cooking with their contents being watched over by her cooking mates. She looked up from her pot and saw what seemed to be her older sister Mrs. Eugenia who was walking hurriedly towards her.

"Sister, how did you find me?"

"It was the children who directed me here."

"I know you cannot be here unless for a reason," she said half not wanting to hear as it always seemed there was no bad news to learn.

"I have just this moment seen that Regina left this morning with her friend Micheal.

The young man, you know, the one who used to come form her school to visit her."

Comfort was unsure of the meaning of the statement, and with a bewildered look asked, "What do you mean she has left with her friend? Left for where?"

Her sister insisted "She has gone, this morning I found her gone with her load and she left a note saying that she has run away to marry the young man."

"I know of him, but last I asked you told me that you had not seen him and that she was determined to continue forward with this marriage to the Chief, and now you say this young man has come back".

"I do not know I have a letter; she has left the ring and the dress to be returned to the Chief."

Comfort who was standing in the heat of the sun over the pot swooned, and then she felt her knees buckle under her, and if not for the swift response of her sister, she would have fainted right into the pot of bubbling stew, instead she was steered clear of the fire and assisted to the ground . She lay on her back with her head in her sisters laps ,her sister was fanning her on her face, " Comfort,wake up, wake up ",

She woke up and stuttered,

"No, I do not want to wake up; I want to go to the hospital. In fact take me to the hospital right now as I cannot face Moses this time, I will not be the one to give him this news."

And so it befell upon Mrs. Eugenia to become the harbinger of the bad news to Moses at home.

As it was a Thursday holiday he was seated on a bench in front of the compound with some of his friends and they were enjoying a lazy afternoon with palm wine and beer and some cola nuts being shared around by the men who were relatives from Moses village, who had come to town for the wedding which was to take place the next day at the courthouse.

A stray dog was nosing his way through a near by pile of garbage which served as the area garbage dump.

As she neared the group she was met by a young boy with a set of rosary beads around his neck and dirty brown shorts, in his left hand he carried a stick and he was carefully running down the hill beside her guiding a wheel of an old bicycle in a familiar game played by the boys in town. His eyes were quite oblivious of all around him and he was intent on maintaining the wheel upright with his stick and the gravity pulling the wheel down the hill. Carefully he negotiated his ways past the gullies and vanished behind a curve. The conversations on the bench under the tree which were being conducted in perfect Igbo, seized upon the arrival of the woman, and Mr. Moses who was in a jovial mood stood up to greet his sister in law initially with a smile, but when he noticed the smile went unreturned and that she was motioning for him to follow her he excused himself from the group and went with her into the inner courtyard for some privacy. She brought out the note and handed it to him

For a moment he was close to accusing the woman for all this, then he took hold of himself and said instead,

"Mrs. Eugenia, you had no idea of this? You had reassured me that after I rejected the young man you never saw him again"
"And that was true, I never saw him again."
"So who will tell the chief? Who will tell my wife?
It was then decided that one of the cousins from out of town would break the news to the chief at his hotel.

Early the next morning Moses was rushed to the University of Nigeria Teaching Hospital via ambulance. He was unconscious having drunk himself into a stupor in the early hours of the morning. he was too weak to get out of the bed. and in the meantime his father came from the village to check on his son .
The father was horrified and he asked repeated questions of the doctor who said that he was treating Moses for exhaustion and malaria, and did not believe a word the doctor said. So the next day he hurriedly returned to their town and he went to visit the village medicine man to find out what really could have gone so wrong, for his grand daughter to have run away, and for his son to be dying in the hospital.
The dibia was an old man and he was in his hut wearing a wrapper and a tee shirt and he had his magical pouch with him that contained all manner of feathers and stones and potions he started with his incantations and after a while he seemed to enter a trance and started to hold conversations with people who were not present and all manner of things were moving on their own in the room. At one point there was a rope which he had held up which was now hanging freely on it's own in the air, suspended defiant of gravity. He threw his stones up in the air and drew marks with his magical sticks and then came the verdict that the problem was from the family of the dead mother of Moses. Apparently Moses had failed to give honor to the family of his dead mother for the successes of his trade. He then went on to ask the native man to tell him about his daughter the runaway Regina. This was followed by a blank look, and the medicine man said he could not find Regina, nor could he find the purported husband Michael.
He was told that he must go the market place to buy a chicken for sacrifice and that it would be a specific white chicken and that when he got to the market he would know which chicken it was. On

arrival at the marketplace as he and his son were walking around the chickens, all of a sudden a white chicken jumped up high in the air and stayed up crowing loud and flapping its wings frantically, crow crow.

"That is the one," the father shouted. And the poultry seller tied the legs of the wildly flapping chicken together, which had singled itself out as the one for the ungodly sacrifice. The chicken was placed alive in a sack and they returned to the dibia, who took the chicken and walked with them on a bush path to outside the town, where the throat of the chicken was cut with a knife and the blood was drained on the ground.

At that moment, in Enugu, Moses who had been asleep in his hospital bed woke up for the first time in three days; his fever was gone, and he asked his wife to bring him pepper soup.

From then on his health had returned, and several days later, when he felt well enough, he decided with his cousin to go in pursuit of Regina and Michael. To make matters even more complicated, the only information they had on the young man was that he had been a student of the Agricultural college of Awka, and that he had successfully graduated that year. It was known that his name was Michael, however, Mrs. Regina had never known the boys last name, but had a feeling that his last name was 'Obi'; a more common name could hardly more have been his in Igbo land.

On arrival at the registrars office of the College of Agriculture, he had introduced himself ,only to find out that no one by the name of 'Michael Obi' had ever attended the college. Thus he had then been forced to go the police station and to make a missing persons report in order for the school to agree to open up it's books and assist him in his search, as they were protected by confidentiality laws. It was determined that the only name similar was 'Michael Asimnobi', who hailed from a nearby village, on the outskirts of Awka township and had just graduated.

A visit to Michael Asimnobi's father at his bungalow outside Awka:

With some of the funds at his disposal from the generosity of the chief, he paid a visit to the father of Michael Asimnobi in his retirement in the village. The story of Mr. Asimnobi himself was quite exciting.

Looking upon him as he was seated on the verandah outside his bungalow on the outskirts of Awka it was easy to think of him as yet another retired man who had returned to the land of his ancestors. The bungalow was painted a pale yellow hue, which contrasted beautifully with the deep red color of the surrounding laterite soil; and the house was framed by a lush array of trees: mango, iroko, and palm trees, with great branches all filled with a luxurious thicket of green leaves. This created a shade that provided a natural respite from the heat of the mid day sun. Judging by the diameters of the trunks some of the trees must have been nearly a hundred years old; for this was the compound where his father and his father's father had been born. This was where he had been born, and in this land that he hoped to be buried, right in this compound beside his father. For that was the custom, to bury the dead where the living were living; and in this way there was a natural continuum between life and death, for death was never far off.

 Yet, on speaking to him, it was obvious that Mr. Anthony Asimnobi had known better days. That is not to say that retirement to the village is bad in and of itself. For here, his bungalow was of reasonable size; and not altogether without the comforts of modern life. The structure had elaborate iron bars across all the windows, and due to a strategically placed bore hole had water running in the pipes. Electricity was supplied by a small diesel generator. The furnishings were genteel enough, being the common wooden framed furniture locally made from the local mahogany, with foam cushions placed on top of a set of springs. All this, a stark contrast to the comfortable apartments he had known when working in the Nigerian High Commission in London; but that was before the civil war. Those days, now thirty years prior, to him, sometimes, it seemed as if maybe the London days had never happened; perhaps it was a sick joke of fate to tantalize him with dreams of a past that was just as brief as it had been sweet. Then, he had been recalled, to the Eastern region, and the hostilities had broken out. He could still remember the day of the declaration of independence; he was in Enugu that day. What uncharacteristic unity had united them then, displayed ever so temporally and perhaps never to be seen again, at least not in his own lifetime, with the soldiers driving around in jeeps waving palm fronds, like the Jews had done on the triumphant entry of Jesus into Jerusalem. But that was before the starvation and death that followed in its wake. He had of course proceeded to loose everything, just as everyone else did, every stick of furniture was removed from his house after his return; indeed the devastation left in its wake by the federalist forces was ominous; so potent and effective had their plundering been of the vanquished areas that what could not be carted off in lorries, was burnt. He had lost his three brothers, and his career in the diplomatic service had come to an abrupt halt, and not even the rendition of General Yakubu Gowon, that there was "No victor and no vanquished", could reinstate him in the diplomatic service. The sense of loss was real. But those were all things and careers, and things could be replaced, but his brothers' could not. And it was this fact that left him with a tinge of bitterness in his soul, a scar which would remain with him until the day he died. During the civil war he had been in the cabinet of General Odumegwu Ojukwu, and he had spent the first two years after the war under house arrest by the federalist forces. After his release, he had stayed on in the village, and had farmed his lands to survive. And it was to this Biafran war time hero that the humble Mr. Moses Okafor had to present himself whilst in search of his daughter. Mr. Moses Okafor himself was a veteran of the war, and he instantly recognized the face that went with the name. Having fought in the 'xxth' battalion he was no stranger to suffering; narrowly escaping death on multiple occasions, and on even more occasions escaping loosing a limb, and belonging to the dispossessed soldiers at the war camp of Oji River.

He walked in slowly after being announced by the steward, who had been reluctant to admit him into the compound in the first place, as Mr. Moses could not concisely state his mission.

"State your mission sir." He was told, as he approached the chairs on the verandah. This was followed by the usual preamble amongst war veterans, about who was who, and who had fought where, and about who had died, and who had lived.

Then, Mr. Anthony Asimnobi stated emphatically:

"No more war, no never, no more war."

And in these few words he summarized the hopes of his people, who had never even in their wildest dreams imagined what destruction could happen in a twentieth century war. This was not in an effort to pretend that the peoples were not a warlike tribe; no, in all probability, all the towns had known of some war or the other, or of their grand fathers fighting against a neighboring town over some dispute. But the scope had been different, for in those wars one or two bodies were brought back and it was a lot. No, with the arrival of the colonialists had come the efficient machinery of war; and in it's wake, the interplay of international powers, who felt it their duty to side with whom they pleased, and the one or two dead escalated a million fold.

"No more war," Mr. Moses echoed after him, "But it is not the war I have come to talk about, I have come to find my daughter, whom my sister in law states, has written a letter, to say, that she has eloped with your son Michael."

The father appeared stupefied and then he thoughtfully responded, "Michael?" the man asked, "Hum, Michael has mentioned no lady friend to me, no fiancé either. So I do not understand why you are saying all this. In fact, how can he marry, a student just graduated? He has no job, no money either."

"That was just what I thought," Moses replied drily.

It was thus quickly assessed that the young man had not returned home with Regina; and that the boy's father had never heard of her, or of Mrs. Eugenia, or of Moses either. He knew that his son had finished his degree, and that he was about to start Youth Service corps, and that the boy was 'waiting for his posting'. The boy had told the father that he was spending time with a friend in Benin, but the father did not know who the friend was, nor of where he lived.

 Mr. Moses Okafor was quickly becoming exasperated,

"You know, sir," he had said with all sincerity, "I may not be a rich man, but I deserve better than this; I must find my daughter. I cannot rest until I know that she is safe. Yet, you tell me you have no idea where to look for your son; surely you must have some ideas about who his friends are, or where he might have gone. How can I appeal to you as a father, a brother? Please help me!"

Mr. Asimnobi was affected by the man's candor, and promised to assist him in anyway he could. And he reassured the man, that no matter his son' failings, he was not a dangerous man and would do the girl no harm.

And so it came about that Moses had to leave and return without Regina, as there was nothing more he could do. He could ill afford to be off work, and most certainly could not afford to travel all over the country in search of his daughter, as this was equivalent to looking for a needle in a hay stack. He trusted she was fine; and on his return , feeling somewhat reassured about his daughters safety, he sent a letter to the Chief, explaining that the situation was now out of his hands, and the marriage was off for good.

It was a usual evening with Mrs. Eugenia Nwafor:

The Christmas holidays were over, and all the children had returned to school.
Mr. Moses Okafor had returned without Regina, and indeed with no more information in regards to the girl, other than that she presumably was somewhere in Benin with the young Michael Asimnobi. Mr. Moses felt that having met the young man himself, and having been reassured by Mrs Eugenia that this man was one of the finest. The family could rest at ease that Regina was safe.
 Perhaps, the economic hardships they had endured would continue for the time being, but Comfort was still strong, and could work the stall and the catering. The widow Mrs. Oby Chijioke had come for dinner, and the two were watching the sun set over the Milliken hills from two chairs on the small balcony overlooking Chime Avenue. A cool breeze of evening air was coming in; and as the darkness quickly descended over Enugu, Mrs. Chijioke's driver emerged from the car, and waved to his madam that it was time to go before it became too late.

After her friend had left she sat down and drank a cup of hot tea.

A lot had happened over the past year, she thought to herself, as she sat by the café style table; and she thought about how everything was now so different from her dreams and her hopes. Then she remembered that there was much to be thankful for, and that as long as there was life, there was hope. True, if she had had the chance to have been the master of her own destiny, she would have written it to have had a happy ending; for her weakness had been to only read happy books, and watch happy movies.

In essence, in her subconscious, she had relentlessly pursued this very happiness that had eluded her. She remembered how papa had laughed at her when she was young, and she had said she wanted to be happy always, and he had replied that "if wishes were horses then beggars would ride." And she smiled to herself, for so well had her situation improved, that she could now smile to herself, and said, "I may not any longer have a husband, through no fault of my own, and society may well castigate me for this," and she took a deep breath and pulled her shoulders back with a rediscovered self confidence, and a gentle smile lingered on her lips…. "And in this rejection, I shall find my salvation; and one day, joy will return to my soul".

It was quickly assessed that the young man had not returned home with Regina, and in fact, the boy's father had never heard of Regina, nor of Mrs. Eugenia, nor even of Moses either. He knew that his son had finished his degree and that he was to start his youth service corps, but the boy was still waiting for his posting, and had told his father he was going to spend some time with a friend in Benin but the father did not know the friends name nor where he lived.
" You know, sir, I may not be a rich man, but I deserve better than this, I must find my daughter, I cannot.

Mrs. Eugenia returns to Enugu after spending Christmas in Lagos:

The harmattan came late that year, and by the time the family was to return to Enugu, a swarm of dust had descended on the southern part of the country making the air heavy with dust; the sun was barely visible as a round shiny disc far in the distance. The Lagos airport was forced to close and the flights had to be diverted, and the offices of the luxury coaches serving Eastern Nigeria were overflowing with passengers. The family was lucky to still get a seat and started the long ride home to Enugu.

MRS EUGENIA NWAFOR: WAS MARRIED TO MR. CHRISTIAN NWAFOR, whom she left on the day of his tradiotional wedding to Henrietta his mistress of 16 years.
Children:
#1: Chinedu.
#2. Afam.
#3. Henrietta.
#4. Christiana.
MRS Henrietta Nwafor: Misstress who becomes the second wife of Christian.

MARGARET OBIORA: YOUNGER SISTER OF MRS EUGENIA, MARRIED TO CHARLES OBIORA A PROSPEROUS LAGOS TRADER with a branch in Onitsha main market.
Five children.
Three children are attending the Ambassador school in Enugu.

COMFORT THE YOUNGEST SISTER OF MRS.EUGENIA, LIVES IN A ONE BEDROOM IN ASATA WITH her husband Moses and five children.

Regina: the first child engaged to Chief Obi of the U.S.

Michael: The agricultural student whom Regina truly is in love with.

MR AND MRS SAMUEL OKAFOR 9deceased, parents of the 3 ladies.

MRS CHIJIOKE: the widow of MR.PAUL CHIJIOKE and the best friend of MRS Eugenia.

The Plot:

The newly weds: Henrietta and Charlie.
Regina and Michael the love affair.
The love child of Henrietta and Christian.
Margaret and Charlie in Lagos.
Can Regina elope and run away with Michael?

Lets do it:

Mrs Chijioke had just returned from her annual trip to Lagos.
She had barely finished her bucket bath when her maid was
knocking on the door.
" Madam. please can you come to the parlour and see Mrs
Eugenia right away as she says she has an urgent mesage for
you."
Mrs Chijioke was alarmed. She quickly put on a Boo boo and
went as quickly as she could to the parlour. On her arrival she
found Mrs Eugenia Nwafor seated in the Love seat. Her hair
was disshevelled form the preceding days activities and she
sat motionless with a dazed gaze looking into space deep in
thought. Beside her stood her trunk, suitcase and carboard
box as telltale signs of her fate. Mrs Chijioke came in, and
sensing that something must be very amiss she gently placed
her hand on her friends shoulder before saying ever so softly.
" Tell me Mrs Eugenia, is this all your load? What is the
matter?"
" Christian has married Henrietta", was the simple reply given.
" I thought as much' her friend answered Oh dear I must admit
that for long I had suspected that something like that might
happen." Her friend replied.
" Yet, Mrs Chijioke, you never said this to me, or aything
evenly close
please plan as follows:

Mrs Eugenia at Mrs chijiokes house the first night
then elaborate more on the post divorce trauma
further regina and michael elope.
more on regina and chief Obi.
Need to have more on Christian and Henrietta?

More on the children.
A holiday in lagos.

Mrs Eugenia Nwafor burst into tears, a flood gate of tears poured dow her cheeks, as all the emotions of the last few days finally overcame her.

" Ewo, Ewo me" Ka ngwa gi ! Chukwu na me, chukwu na me" She wailed " Why me? When I walked down the aisle I was the happiest bride east of the River Niger! Then you know, I do not know or understand how or why this happened? But I can tell you for the last ten years we have lived under the shadow of Henrietta."

Now tell me what exactly happened. Was it Christin who asked you to leave?"

" Actully no" She replied, not understanding the apparent relevance everyone except herself placed upon this little detail. For all she knew or card the effect was the same, and that was that she was now no longer in her marital home an never would be again.

Then she continued, " I moved out without being asked when I found out that the following day he had scheduled his traditional wedding to Henrietta."

Her friend's face lit up,

" How brave of you! I wish that all women could see this example of courage."

Her friend seemed surprised to hear this and asked shyly,

" Do you truely think it a courageous act to leave your husband or are you just saying so for my sake? What about it mkes it courageous?"

" I think it is the courage to stand up for the truth and for your beliefs. What beliefs, you may ask. But Christianity of course. And no matter how the men may want to tweak it, we repudiated polygamy with the advent of christianity, no? Yet so many of our men pick and choose what pleases them from christianity and our traditional beliefs. I think that is a sham."

Mrs Eugenia Nwafor breaks down:

" Sometimes, I feel like I have descended into this dark tunnel, or depression if you will. It is a situation over which I am totally powerless. My heart is broken. I say to myself, even in this rejection I must find my salvation. Like all trials sent by divine providdence they are not ones of our own choosing, rather what God has seen fit to send us. Of all the sorrows in the world

The plot:
Regina breaks up and is forced to reinstate her engagement by moses.
Michael continues to meret her in secret qat okpara square.
They finally elope when chief returns for the wedding.
Eugenia looses her job
Comfort faints at party while cooking when told of elopement of regina
More on christyian and Henrietta.
Mrs Eugenia on vacation in lagos.

At the home of Mr. Moses and Mrs. Comfort Okafor in Asata the news of the broken engagement.

I have quite fallen in love with the characters in the story myself, and I find myself asking what happens next, and I am nearly pulled in to their little flats and their little minds. Their worlds are so small and yet so big in the sense of the goodness that they carry in their souls, at least the heroine. I think at this point I have one diesire only and that is to finish this story and to move on to the next, in my usual fickleness I get bored so quickly and cannot resist the desire to move on,in may ways I think I must have some form of ADD. Comfort was standing above the large cast black cast iron pot in which bubbled a large red stew which was steaming up into the air. She was singing a song and stirring her pot with wanton abandon, on the other side of the compound there were two other pots with their contents being watched over by her cooking mates. She looked up from her pot and saw what seemed to be her older sister Mrs. Eugenia who was walking hurriedly towards her.

www.ingramcontent.com/pod-product-compliance
Lightning Source LLC
Chambersburg PA
CBHW070531130626
46555CB00003B/1366